D1520350

SEDUCING THE
Bridesmaid

A WEDDING DARE NOVEL

KATEE ROBERT

Entangled Publishing, LLC
2614 South Timberline Road
Suite 109
Fort Collins, CO 80525
Visit our website at www.entangledpublishing.com.

Brazen is an imprint of Entangled Publishing, LLC. For more information on our titles, visit www.brazenbooks.com.

Edited by Heather Howland and Ellie Brennan
Cover design by Heather Howland

Manufactured in the United States of America

First Edition June 2014

To Tim. This one's for you, babe.

Chapter One

Brock McNeill had never been all that good at turning down trouble. And the brunette leaving Spago right now had trouble written all over her.

He should just let her go. After all, the only reason he was at Beaver Creek Resort in the first place was because of his childhood friend's wedding. He was here to support Colton—not to cozy up to any of the bridesmaids.

Especially *this* bridesmaid.

Regan Wakefield, sorority sister to the bride, headhunter, and wearer of six-inch heels. At dinner, she'd stood out among the other women like a bird of paradise among swans. And there was something *there*. Something about how she held herself aloof even when drinking and chatting with her friends, her eyes taking in everything around her. It didn't help that she had the kind of beauty that could bring a man to his knees—or that she seemed to know it.

Damn it, he couldn't just let her walk back to the hotel

alone.

Brock threw back the rest of his drink and dropped a twenty on the bar. He pushed through the exterior door and looked around. She was already fifty yards down the paved path, her heels clicking as she strolled through the night. He'd figured those torture devices on her feet would slow her down. Apparently he'd been wrong.

"Wait up." She didn't even look over her shoulder, so he picked up his pace, mentally cursing the stupid dress shoes pinching his toes. "Regan."

If he hadn't been watching her so closely, he wouldn't have noticed the way her shoulders tightened up. She turned, raked him with a single glance, and kept going. "Sorry, but my granny told me not to talk to strangers."

"I'm not a stranger." He finally came even with her and slowed down to match her walk.

She flipped her dark hair over her shoulder. "You're not?" She snapped her fingers. "Oh wait, aren't you that guy—"

"You know damn well who I am." He and the other groomsmen had had drinks in the same damn bar as the bridesmaids last night, and they'd all been at dinner tonight. This woman, of all people, wasn't going to forget a face. He smiled at her, turning on the charm.

She laughed, glanced back at his face, and laughed harder. "Oh my God."

What the fuck? Did he have spinach in his teeth? Brock resisted the urge to cover his mouth, but only barely. He waited as they kept walking, but she didn't stop laughing. Christ, what was the deal with this woman? "What's so funny?"

She finally managed to contain her mirth, though her dark eyes still danced. "You." She waved her hand at his entire body. "Turning on the Southern panty-dropper charm. It's adorable."

Adorable. He'd been called a lot of things in his life—charming, gorgeous, a fuckup—but never that. Grown men were not adorable. *Puppies* were adorable. "I don't know what you're talking about."

"Sure you do. I bet you practice that smile in the mirror."

She thought she had his number down. It stung more than it should because he *did* pride himself on his charm. "Naw, darlin'. I'm all natural."

"That's what they all say. Run along now. I don't have time for you."

He couldn't remember the last time he'd been so thoroughly dismissed, though Brock could bet it was his father who'd done it. "That's going to be a problem."

She didn't look at him. "How so?"

"In the South, we don't let women wander alone at night. It's dangerous. I'll walk you back to the hotel."

"You don't let women wander alone, huh? God forbid one of those belles escapes her caretaker." She clutched her hands to her chest and affected a pretty damn good accent. "Alone? With no strong man to protect me? Whatever shall I do?"

"That's not what I meant and you know it."

"How do I know it? I'm not a mind reader, and I don't need some strapping man to walk me the hundred yards from here to the hotel when I'm in a damn resort. I live in New York. There's nothing out here that can compare to that."

"That makes sense."

As expected, she gave him a suspicious look. "You're

being awfully agreeable all of a sudden."

He kept his smile in place and went in for the kill. "Only because you're the scariest thing within twenty miles."

She flinched, but recovered almost immediately. "Maybe you're smarter than I thought."

"And you're sneakier than I expected. Want to tell me what that key switch you pulled last night was all about?" His friend Reed had looked pretty damn shell-shocked this morning so he suspected Regan's plan had been successful. "Some kind of friend you are, sending that nice Southern girl to the wrong room."

She shrugged. "She had her sights set on the wrong man."

The sheer size of the balls on this woman blew him away. "How is that any of your damn business? That was some sneaky shit and you know it."

"She's my friend and I want to see her happy." She picked up her pace, but he kept up easily. "There's nothing I wouldn't do to see my friends happy."

He could admire the sentiment, even if her methods were suspect. "Then why not just, I don't know, open your mouth and say something? You don't seem to have a problem shoving your opinion down people's throats. Mine, for instance."

"*You* chased my ass out here. I didn't ask for help."

Yeah, he didn't get the idea that she asked for help all that often—or ever. "Maybe you should."

She laughed. "Because you're going to be the one to save me from myself, right? For at least as long as it takes to get into my pants."

Well, hell. He wouldn't mind getting into her pants—or up her skirt, as it were. But she wasn't even going to give him a chance. He could trot along, verbally sparring, or he could change the game. Brock slid in front of her, blocking her way. "Darlin', if I didn't know better, I'd say you were thinking about sexing me up."

Her eyebrows rose, though he didn't miss the way her gaze coasted over his body. "It's a good thing one of us knows better then, isn't it?"

"It's okay that you're scared. You've never met a man like me."

It was hard to tell in the dark, but he thought he could see a blush spreading across her chest. Until she laughed in his face. "Please. There are a thousand men like you. But it's cute that you think you're so special. Did your mother tell you that?"

There had been enough praise in the McNeill household for only one son, and Brock wasn't him. But he wasn't about to say as much to Regan. She was a shark, and she'd sniff out any weakness and exploit it without a second thought. He'd never found ruthlessness particularly attractive in a woman, but combined with her sharp tongue, it was an intriguing mix.

He leaned in and lowered his voice. "It's okay that you're intimidated by my overwhelming masculinity. I promise to take good care of you."

"How sweet of you." She walked her fingers up his chest, inch by slow inch, the briefest contact that sent heat pulsing through his body. Regan stopped at the hollow of his throat and smiled.

Then she flicked his chin. "But let's be honest. I'd ruin you for other women, and I'm just too nice to do that to an *adorable* little thing like you."

"Yeah, I don't think so."

"Maybe in another life. You're hot, but pretty is as pretty does." She stepped around him and headed for the hotel, trailing her perfume behind her. He closed his eyes and inhaled—something expensive, subtle, and intriguing. Too bad the woman herself was only two of those three.

He turned and followed, catching up to her in two large steps. "I'm not that easily ruined."

"You haven't been with me." She glanced at him and then jerked back to look straight ahead. "And you aren't going to be."

Then why did she sound like she was trying to convince herself? He watched her as they walked, and sure enough, she shot another look at him a few steps later. For all her bluster, the woman could barely keep her eyes off him. "You just can't help yourself, can you?"

"You're dangerously delusional."

He laughed. "And you're not as mean as you pretend to be."

She stopped just outside of the light cast by the hotel lamps on either side of the door and glared at him, her hands on her hips. "As delightful as this has been, I can take it from here. I don't need a white knight and I sure as hell don't need you to try to charm my panties off." She turned and walked to the door. "Besides, I'm not wearing any." Her last comment floated over her shoulder, almost taking him out at the knees.

Holy shit.

Brock rubbed his hand over his mouth. If he had half a brain, he'd stay as far away from Regan as possible for the rest of the week. She thought she had him all figured out, and he had enough of that shit in his life without adding yet another person who'd be continually reminding him of what a fuckup he supposedly was.

He grinned. On the other hand, it would be a hell of a lot of fun to poke at her and see what lay beneath the polished and poised exterior. Who was he kidding? He was going to seek her out again the first chance he got.

· · ·

Twenty-four hours into this destination wedding, and Regan Wakefield wasn't sure if she was the greatest friend ever—or the worst.

She leaned against the bar and stared into her drink. It had started last night at the bachelorette party. She could blame the dare on the alcohol, the altitude, or the seriously hot choice of groomsmen, but the end result was a promise to hook up with one of said groomsmen this week. Her sorority sister Julie had thought it was a brilliant idea, and both Christine and the groom's sister, Sophie, had gone along with it. More or less. Regan had agreed at the time—a no-brainer since she had come up with the idea.

That was before that smart-ass Brock had shown up and tried to charm her while she made her way back to the hotel. He was the groomsman who wasn't Sweet, wasn't Brooding, and wasn't the Full Package. The one who practically reeked of Old Money and the life of ease that came with it. He'd riled her up so much, she hadn't been able to bear the thought of heading back to her room alone. So she'd come here, to the same bar they'd all been in last night.

She tended to be excellent at reading people and situations.

Her reputation as a headhunter depended on recommending the right people for the right jobs—keeping them in said jobs long enough to get her bonus meant knowing it'd be a good fit going in. And Brock wasn't even close to acceptable.

No, what she needed was a strong and steady man who'd be a partner. The dare might have been aimed at more temporary fun, but if she could kill two birds with one stone… Well, Regan was all about more bang for her buck.

Logan, the best man, was the kind of man who'd meet both needs. He was classically handsome, driven enough to be CEO of his own climbing company, and generally seemed like a nice guy. *He* was the one she had set her sights on.

That was before she'd pulled the ballsy move of switching the room keys on Julie last night, though, sending her to the wrong room to seduce the wrong man. Or the *right* one, if Regan was right—and she was *always* right when it came to reading people. It had been a spur-of-the-moment impulse she couldn't deny. But when her best friend said she had her eyes set on Logan, Regan had seen it for the mistake it was—and *not* because he was the only one she considered suitable. The man was great, but no man was great enough to sever a friendship between her and one of her girls. Chicks before dicks, and all that.

But as much as Julie liked to kill herself aiming for perfection, she needed someone to balance her out. Mister Danger, Reed, fit the bill. He was dark, gorgeous, and brooding. The kind of guy who needed a bright spot in his life as desperately as Julie needed someone who could look beneath the surface and call her out for putting everyone else first.

Regan shook her head and took the shot—her favorite,

a Short Southern Screw—she'd just ordered. It didn't matter. There was no point obsessing over what she could or should have done. She'd done it and, by the time she finished her little switch, Logan was nowhere to be seen. The upside was that Julie hadn't gone for her eyes today at dinner, so *that*, at least, must have all worked out well enough.

Turning to survey the rest of the room, she propped her elbows on the bar. It was a damn shame Logan had left the party at Spago earlier and didn't appear to be planning on making an appearance at the bar tonight. The man was seriously hard to pin down.

Oh well. The night was young and she hadn't had a real vacation in two years. She might as well enjoy herself. She motioned to the bartender. "Another one, please."

"I hate to be the one to tell you this, darlin', but you're setting your sights too low." The Southern drawl rolled through her like the best kind of bourbon, making a small feminine part of her swoon in delight.

It was a good thing she wasn't ruled by such stupid impulses, especially when she knew exactly whom that voice belonged to. Regan glanced over, careful to school any expression from her face. "You again? I thought I'd made myself clear when I left you staring after me outside the hotel half an hour ago. Besides, if you paid attention, you'd realize I *never* set my sights too low."

"A Short Southern Screw? So I *was* right. You're craving something south of the Mason-Dixon Line." He moved closer, crowding her even though there was still a good twelve inches between them. "I can assure you, though, I'm a man who isn't short in any sense of the word."

Holy shit, he blew right past self-confidence and overshot

arrogance by a mile. She held up three fingers, dropping them one at a time. "Arrogant. Playboy. *Ass*."

"You know, I heard you do that neat little trick of summing people up." He didn't look all that torn up about it. What a shame. "Darlin', you'll need a whole lot more than three words for me."

She smiled, well aware it wasn't a nice expression. Unlike this guy, she'd done her research before she got on the plane from NYC. It was how she'd narrowed down her options to Logan within five minutes of seeing Colton's group of friends. "Brock McNeill. Good friend to Reed Lawson. Grew up with Kady's soon-to-be husband, Colton. From a wealthy family down in Tennessee and is the favored younger son. So I guess you're right—I should add lazy and rudderless to that list."

Instead of storming off in a huff like she'd hoped, a slow grin spread over his face. And what a face it was. His tanned skin hinted at countless hours spent in the sun—or possibly some exotic lineage. It wasn't the almost-too-long dark hair or the hazel eyes that made her stomach drop, though. It was that damn smile. Wide and white and bracketed by laugh lines. Even his eyes lit up, as if this were a man who knew how to enjoy the pleasures life offered.

God, what was she thinking? He probably *did* practice that grin in the mirror. Regan made a shooing motion with her hand. "Go on now, Scarlett. I already have a drink." *Did I seriously just call him Scarlett? As in Scarlett O'Hara? What the hell is wrong with me?*

"I might be pretty, but I don't have the shoulders to pull off a hoop skirt."

Brock turned to the bartender, giving her the opportunity

to eyeball the way his button-up white shirt hugged said shoulders and, holy shit, those back muscles were nothing to sneeze at. He'd gotten rid of the suit jacket he'd been wearing during their walk, and the tucked-in shirt only served to accent his slim hips and an ass that probably had lesser women salivating. Because she most certainly wasn't. Much.

She'd gotten herself under control by the time he turned around, but it was a close thing. For his part, his grin hadn't slipped. "Generally when a fella asks to buy a lady a drink, she doesn't respond so vehemently."

Probably not when *he* asked.

She'd dealt with Southern good ol' boys more than once in her line of business, and she'd never been anything but cool and professional. Fifteen minutes alone with this man and she alternately wanted to slap that grin off his face and bite his shoulders. *Get a hold of yourself.* She took the offered drink. "I heard you had a reputation with the *ladies*." It wasn't exactly true. But she didn't have to be a genius to realize most women would have problems being in the same room with this man without throwing themselves at him. As hot as he was, she'd never been a fan of being one of the faceless masses.

Brock leaned against the bar, entirely too close. "You seem to have heard a lot."

"You have no idea."

"I'd like to."

Regan took another sip of her drink, only now registering that it was a cosmopolitan. One of her favorites. Obviously he'd been watching her for longer than she'd realized before rushing out to play her knight in Gucci armor. She propped a hip on the bar. "I bet you don't hear *no* a lot."

"It's a dirty word. I'm not a fan of it."

Of course not. Though he sure as hell was charming, he was also the last person she wanted to be talking to right now. Damn Logan for disappearing when she would have made her move. Yes, Brock was gorgeous, but from what she could figure out from chatting with Kady, he was content to spend his life riding on his daddy's coattails. The man was more charm than substance.

"If you're looking for some company, I know just the man for the job." He leaned forward, his grin widening. "And he doesn't have a problem with short screws."

She just bet he didn't. She needed to get rid of him. Now. "It just so happens that I'm looking for my friend Christine." She'd been really quiet since they showed up here yesterday, and teasing aside, Regan was worried about her. Quiet tended to be Christine's gig, but something had changed. She wasn't happy. It might be the upcoming move to Maine throwing her off, but Regan didn't think so.

"The little redhead? I think I saw Kady's brother follow her out of Spago."

Tyler? Now *that* was interesting. Maybe the torch Christine had been carrying for years wasn't one she was carrying alone.

She shook her head. She couldn't afford to get distracted with potential pair-ups when Brock was right in front of her, taking too much space. He exerted an almost magnetic pull, so strong it was an effort not to take that last step between them and see if his muscles felt as good as they looked. From the way the women around them were staring, she wasn't the only one feeling that urge.

That realization shocked her back to herself. He was working her, plain and simple. This man was used to getting what he wanted, and right now he had his sights set on her. She couldn't afford to get caught up in this.

Could she?

No, that was a bad idea. Regan knew bad ideas. They always started out sounding really reasonable and totally logical and, next thing she knew, she was half a bottle of tequila in and riding a mechanical bull in a miniskirt. Or spending a whole six weeks dating that douche Danny Levitz because he had lickable abs. Or… The list went on and on.

"Come on, darlin'."

"There will be no coming on anything."

"Killjoy."

"Look at you and your fancy words. Your daddy must be so proud."

Brock's grin dimmed, but he reclaimed it almost instantly. "A week without is enough to make anyone cranky. I can only imagine what it would make *you*."

She gave in to the urge to give his biceps a squeeze. The tense muscles beneath her hand almost made her groan. The man obviously spent an inordinate amount of time in the gym. She could appreciate that, even if the personality it represented was less than impressive. "Why, Scarlett, are you calling me difficult? I seem to remember you making irrational claims about my not being as mean as I acted." *Take that, you arrogant ass.*

"God, no. I'm just pointing out that you have a mammoth stick up your ass." He reached for his drink, effectively removing her hand from his arm. "Since I'm petitioning for saintly status, I'm willing to help you remove it."

She set the glass down a little harder than necessary. "That's not a stick, but it only makes sense that someone as rudderless as you wouldn't recognize ambition if it slapped you in the face."

He gave her a knowing grin. "Try me. The offer's still on the table."

God, was there no dissuading this guy? Normally, this level of dogged determination would be enough for her to dump her cosmo on his head and march out the door. "You want me to tie you up and make you call me Daddy? Maybe a little whips and chains and handcuffs. Why, Scarlett, I am positively *shocked*."

He pushed the shot she'd just ordered toward her. "I'm just offering up something you desperately need. Like I said—I'm practically a saint for being willing to shoulder that burden."

Sleeping with her was a *burden*. Even knowing he was trying to get a rise out of her, the she-devil on her shoulder made her want to push Brock over the edge and make him beg for mercy. Julie had always said that imaginary little bitch was going to get her into trouble, and Regan was beginning to think she was right.

She took her shot. "You're really that eager to be ruined."

"I think you'll be surprised." He didn't touch her, didn't move to close that last few inches between them, didn't do a damn thing but lean against the bar and watch her, but her body heated under those dark eyes. He was looking at her like she was a sure thing. It had obviously been too long since she'd blown off some steam, because she was seriously considering taking him up on what he was offering.

There was no way he could live up to his talk. In her experience, the men who talked the most had the most to prove. Even knowing that, it was a fight to stop herself from leaning into him. Taking him up on his offer was a stupid idea, she-devil on her shoulder or not.

And she was most definitely going to hell, because she couldn't come up with a single argument to talk herself out of it. Both times they'd talked, he got under her skin in record time. The urge to return the favor was overwhelming her common sense. Truthfully, she didn't even want to fight it.

But, God, she was tired of thinking so much. Of constantly second-guessing herself and her reactions against what the people around her were doing. She was always *on*, and it was exhausting. It was time to work off some of her stress.

Regan finished her drink and set it on the bar, plan firmly in place. One night. No strings attached. No complications. "Let's go."

• • •

Brock stared at her retreating back, wondering if he'd heard her wrong. Driven by curiosity and a healthy dose of anger, he followed Regan through the bar. He didn't bother to keep his eyes off her ass—everything about her, from the snazzy way she dressed to her sky-high pink heels to the calculated sexy tumble of her highlighted dark hair, was designed to draw attention. She knew she looked good, and she flaunted it. He could respect that, which was part of the reason he'd approached her in the first place.

That and the way she'd completely shut him down yesterday, and then again tonight. He'd just been trying to make conversation... Okay, that was a damn lie. When she'd waltzed up to Reed and grinned at him last night, Brock felt like he'd just been struck by lightning. And that was with her barely sparing him a glance when she told him there wasn't a single thing about her that was sweet.

Hell if she wasn't right.

He was rapidly coming to the conclusion that the woman wouldn't know sweet if it bit her in the ass. Who the hell summed up a person with three words? She might have been right—to a point—but then she'd had to keep going and call him rudderless. It was the same argument he'd had time and time again with his father. He sure as fuck didn't want to have it with a near stranger.

Not to mention she was totally off base calling him the favored son. That role had always been—and would always be—Caine's. Brock was born second, and had come in second his entire life. There wasn't a single damn thing he could do to change it, even if he wanted to.

They left the bar, the night crisp despite its being June. Back home, the humidity would be thick enough to cut with a knife and the lightning bugs would be making an appearance right around now. He shook off the strange feeling of homesickness and grabbed her arm. "Hey."

The look she gave him would have made a lesser man feel like he was two inches tall. "What part of 'let's go' do you not understand, Scarlett?"

Christ, she was prickly. He released her arm and crossed his own over his chest. "I'm trying not to jump to conclusions. Spit it out."

"I'm more of a swallowing kind of girl."

Holy hell.

Her grin sent all his blood rushing south. She stepped back and reached up to unbutton her shirt, giving him a flash of purple lace. "That was an invitation, in case you were wondering. So why don't we get this show on the road and inside a room?"

He followed her, moving even though his mind argued that this was a mistake. She already thought he was a piece of shit playboy. Sleeping with her wasn't going to help that belief. But Christ, that didn't stop him from wanting to. "You don't even like me, darlin'."

"Who says that's necessary?" Another button opened, highlighting the swell of her breasts. They were magnificent, and she knew it.

He fought back a growl. Liking the person he slept with *was* necessary to him. He wasn't so goddamn desperate that he'd cozy up to a woman who thought he was a joke. "Most people don't fuck people they dislike."

If he thought she'd flinch at his language, he was sorely mistaken. Regan sidled closer and ran a perfectly manicured nail down his chest. He tensed, waiting for the spice that seemed to come whenever she did something even partially sweet.

"Well, *darlin'*, I fuck who I want to, when I want to. And right now, that's you."

There it was.

Even as he cursed himself for questioning this, he said, "Why?"

"Don't worry your pretty head about it." Before he could question her further, she reached down and cupped him through his slacks, the contact nearly making him moan. "*This* is all I'm worried about right now. My room or yours?"

He stared at her mouth. This was stupid. He should tell her to fuck off and go back into the bar. Sleeping with anyone else would be better than going upstairs with

Regan. It didn't matter if their chemistry was off the charts. She obviously thought he wasn't fit to kiss her bright-pink shoes—and he was going to have to spend the next week in close quarters with her. Even knowing that, he found himself saying, "Mine." At least if they were on his territory, he'd maintain control of the situation.

She went up on her tiptoes and nipped his chin. "Perfect."

Chapter Two

Regan almost felt bad about the confusion on Brock's face when she propositioned him. Almost. But hadn't this been exactly what he was aiming for when he tried to walk her back to the hotel, then moved in on her at the bar? She was just cutting through the bullshit and doing it on *her* terms. It just figured that he wouldn't know what to do with a woman who owned her sexuality instead of falling all over herself to dance around it until he decided to make a first move. She took a step back and crooked a finger at him. "Try to keep up."

She put a little more swing in her walk, well aware of how closely he watched her. The man might be totally unsuitable for dating, but he made her toes curl just by looking at her. From the expression on his face, he was probably more than willing to drag her into some shadow and nail her against the nearest wall. It was too bad she had no intention of handing over the reins tonight.

She was going to fuck that country grin right off his face.

It wasn't until they were in the elevator and he'd pushed the button for his floor that he spoke again. "I don't understand you, darlin'."

"What's to understand?" Even as she grinned at him, she tried to ignore the twinge inside her. There was nothing wrong with having a little fun, but fun wasn't the be-all and end-all it'd been a few years ago. Her flings were few and far between these days, and that wasn't even getting into the last man she'd actually tried to *date*. Hell, she hadn't bothered to pick up a guy at a bar in longer than she cared to remember, and it wasn't as if she could date any of the men she worked with since it'd be a conflict of interest. When she took away the ability to meet people at work and the local watering hole, she didn't have a whole lot left to her.

It wasn't that she wanted a husband and two-point-five kids right now, but she was lonely. And hell, she *did* want to end up with someone before she hit thirty. Her parents were still going strong thirty-five years in, and she was delusional to hold out for a love like that. That said, it would happen on *her* timeline—all part of her plan.

But ever since she'd found out Kady was engaged, the feeling of being unsatisfied had gotten worse. Her friend was moving into the next stage of life, the one where she shared her life with another person. As much as Regan loved her independence, it was her parents she called first when she got good news or nailed an intro interview with a prospective client. She couldn't decide if that was great, or really, really sad.

Hell, with Kady caught up in the frenzy of planning a wedding, Regan had actually put some thought into letting her friend Addison set her up on a couple dates. Addison owned one of the premier matchmaking companies in New York, and she'd been joking about getting Regan involved for years.

That was what her life had come down to? Finding a man through a freaking matchmaking service because she couldn't do it on her own?

"You're thinking awfully hard over there."

Shit. She hadn't meant to be mentally waxing poetic about her shitty personal life. Regan shrugged, hoping he was more concerned with getting up her skirt than inside her head. There was only one reason she was spending any time with Brock, and it didn't have to do with his brains. "Just considering if I'm going to let you get to the bed or take you against the door."

"You kiss your mama with that mouth?"

"Every time I see her." And thinking about her parents was the last thing she wanted to do right now. They'd fought for every scrap of food on their table, and to give their daughter whatever she needed to succeed at life. It didn't take much imagination to guess how different Brock's life had been, born with a silver spoon in his mouth.

She hooked a finger through his belt loop as the doors opened, and towed him into the hall. "Enough with the chitchat. Which room is yours?"

"You know, if I didn't know better, I'd say you just want me for my body." He pulled her to a stop in front of a door near the end of the hallway. As he unlocked it, she cast a glance around, hoping no one from the wedding party happened by. It was that risk that had her shoving Brock into his bedroom—that and she couldn't get enough of the surprised look on his face that showed up every time she did something he wasn't expecting.

As soon as the door shut behind her, she pointed at the rolling chair tucked into the desk. "Take off your shirt and sit."

His eyebrows rose, but he obeyed. "Anyone ever tell you that you're pushy?"

"I prefer *assertive*." She took the opportunity to drink him in. As she'd suspected, he was completely ripped. This was a guy who worked for his physique, though she'd be curious to find out exactly what he did to earn that delicious ridge of muscle over his shoulders. "You're right. You really are pretty."

"That's my line."

He still hadn't figured out that his charm had no place here. This was happening on her terms, because she wanted it to—not because he'd said or done anything to sway her.

Anything except seduce her just by standing there.

She gave herself a little shake. *Show no weakness.* "Here's the deal—you do what I say, when I say it, or I leave."

If anything, his eyebrows rose higher. "Do all your sexual encounters start with negotiations?"

Only the ones she felt in danger of losing control with. Even now Regan had to concentrate on not moving closer to him. She wanted to run her hands over his shoulders and down his arms, to strip naked and let him have her any way he wanted.

Which was exactly the reason she couldn't.

She finished unbuttoning her black top and peeled it off, leaving her only in her white skirt. From the way Brock's gaze dropped to her chest and stayed there, she pegged him for a boob man. Good. She had fantastic breasts. As she started to unzip the side of her skirt, she paused. "You have condoms, right?"

"Nightstand. Top drawer."

Thank God. She turned, letting her skirt drop as she did, and stepped out of it. There was no mistaking the strangled groan he made as she bent over to dig through the drawer. A Bible, a box of condoms, a phone charger, and an e-reader.

Apparently her country boy was the type to unpack as soon as he settled into a hotel room.

She grabbed the condoms. "Magnums. How adorable. You know they make these so even a less-than-average-size guy can wear them and get an ego boost, right?"

He laughed, the sound making her thighs clench together. "Woman, you're as mean as a copperhead. Come here and let's find out if you're as cold-blooded."

Ouch. She toyed with one bra strap, determined not to show how much his comment stung. She *was* mean, and she put a lot of effort into keeping that personality at the forefront. In a dog-eat-dog world, only the strong survived, and women in the corporate world had two prominent options—play up their femininity and never threaten their male colleagues' masculinity, or become even bigger ball-busters than the men were.

She'd always figured there was a time and place for both, though she refused to let anyone steamroll her. She reached back and unclasped her bra. Then she dropped it to the side, leaving her in only her purple silk panties.

Brock swallowed visibly. "Damn."

Even as heat sizzled through her body at his blatant appreciation, she hated herself for the weakness. Of course he thought she was gorgeous—she was standing in front of him mostly naked. It wasn't like he'd actually turn her down once he saw her in the skin.

The question remained—where to go from here? He looked half a second from bursting out of that chair and tossing her on the bed, which meant she needed a solution and fast. She held up a finger. "Stay."

That same slow grin spread over Brock's face. "Ruff."

A giggle burst free before she realized it was coming. "You're ridiculous."

"And I was right when I reckoned you had a sense of humor. We all win."

"Yeah, yeah. Hands on your thighs, palms down."

"How am I supposed to touch you if my hands are on my legs?"

He wasn't, which was the plan. She crossed her arms under her breasts, lifting them to draw his attention there. "I could just as easily put my clothes back on and go find my entertainment elsewhere."

Just like that, all joking was gone from his face. His eyes darkened until they were nearly black—and they hadn't been that far off to begin with. "We'll play things your way— this time."

There wouldn't be a next time.

He followed her instructions, pressing his hands to his thighs. She moved a bit closer. "Remember—you touch me, this ends." Because she'd forget all reason and lose herself completely. This was the type of man who expected that kind of response from his partners, and got it through sheer force of personality. She couldn't let him take control.

Regan went to her knees in front of him, eyeing the way

his hard length pressed against his slacks. "Why don't we just loosen things up a bit?"

"By all means."

She carefully undid his pants and pulled them back to free his cock. *Holy shit.* Apparently he hadn't been joking about the Magnum size. Almost idly, she dragged her thumbnail from his tip to his base. "Impressive." And he was.

He spoke through his teeth. "So glad I pass your inspection."

"Oh Scarlett, I haven't even started inspecting." She palmed his cock, trying to keep from shaking as he filled her hand. She wanted him inside her, and she wanted it now.

Even so, she made them both wait as she worked him, enjoying the way every muscle in his body went tight with each downstroke. He was gorgeous in a raw way so few men were anymore, as much a force of nature as the mountains around this resort.

And he was hers for the night.

Unable to contain herself any longer, she slipped her free hand into her panties and spread her wetness around her clit. She was already ready to take him, but teasing them both was too much fun to pass up. A breathy little moan slipped free as her orgasm built around her, and—

Brock's eyes snapped open. "What are you doing?"

"Don't worry about it." She squeezed him a little tighter as she kept circling her clit, pushing herself closer and closer to release.

He leaned forward. "You're playing with yourself."

No point in denying it. Not when she was so close already. "Yeah."

"Stop."

Fat chance of that happening. She pushed a finger inside herself and hissed out a breath.

"Jesus, Regan. Get up here and let me touch you."

If he did, there'd be no going back. More than that, she wanted to torment him just a little bit, to keep something back. A part of her he could never touch. Her orgasm hit her like a freight truck and she cried out and slumped over his lap. He cursed, but there wasn't a damn thing he could do about it unless he wanted to knock her to the floor and break their bargain.

She loved that he didn't move despite the tension riding through every part of his body. She took a deep breath and pressed a kiss to his stomach. "God, that was good."

"You weren't kidding when you said there was nothing sweet about you. That orgasm should have been *mine*."

For a second she thought he was pissed because she'd come first, but then she looked up and saw the expression on his face. *Holy shit*. He wanted to be the one making her come. The answering heat that rose in her at the realization stoked her desire higher than she thought possible. If she let him, he'd make her come again. Hell, he'd probably wring as many orgasms from her as he could, until she was boneless from pleasure and completely incapable of walking away.

Physically or otherwise.

He might be hotter than the devil, but no one was hot enough to make her lose herself. She couldn't afford it.

She dredged up a grin as she reached behind her for the box of condoms. Regan tore one free and rolled it onto his cock, squeezing him again for good measure. While he was busy groaning, she stood and slid off her panties.

Brock cursed again. "You couldn't have even one

imperfection, could you?"

"Imperfection? Someone's using his Word of the Day app."

"Gotta in order to keep up with fancy pants like you." His dark eyes burned into her. Before she could process his intentions, he grabbed her hips and pulled her onto him. The feeling of those big hands on her skin had her biting back the need to beg him to keep touching her until she forgot all the reasons why this was a terrible idea.

She went rigid. Regan did a lot of things but she never, *ever* begged.

He coasted one hand up her spine to cup the back of her neck. "Kiss me, darlin'."

She wanted to. God, she wanted to. His lips were a breath away, and too tempting by half. She could almost feel them on her skin...

"*No*." If she let him kiss her, she'd lose what little control she had left. It might be very *Pretty Woman* of her, but she didn't believe in kissing her flings. It was too personal, opening up too many vulnerabilities he didn't have a right to. She grabbed his wrists and moved his hands off her body. If one touch could make her forget herself... She couldn't risk it happening again. "Keep your hands to yourself and stick to the plan, Scarlett. Otherwise, I walk."

Something she needed to forcibly remind herself—this man had no place in her life plans.

Chapter Three

Brock couldn't decide if he was pissed or too turned on to care. Regan hadn't molded to any of his initial expectations, taking charge as soon as they got to his room instead of letting him get his hands on her. Looking back, he should have seen it coming from how she'd turned the tables on him at the bar, but it was too late to worry about it now that she had a hold of his wrists and that strange look on her face. Because she *would* leave if he touched her again. She was too damn stubborn not to follow through on that threat.

The way her hands shook told all he needed to know. He wasn't getting that kiss—not now. But the thought of doing it affected her more than the orgasm she'd just stolen from him. She wanted that kiss—probably as desperately as he did. She just wouldn't allow either of them to have it.

Brock vowed right then and there that he'd get his lips on hers and her at *his* mercy before Colton and his woman said "I do" this weekend.

"Now, behave yourself, Scarlett, and I'll give you a treat."

"Darlin', I never behave myself."

She trailed her hands back up to his shoulders. "I'm counting on it." As he strained not to touch her and break his word—again—she reached between them and pressed his cock to her entrance. "See, this isn't so bad."

He met her gaze as she sank onto his length, her wet sheath wrapping around him until it was everything he could do to keep his eyes open. She sighed, the sound so sweet he nearly did a double take.

She began to move, sliding torturously slowly up his cock and back down again. On every downstroke, that sound came out of her mouth, the one that made him want to wrap his arms around her and never let go.

Shit, what the hell was wrong with him?

She gripped his shoulders, using the leverage to move more frantically. Her breasts caught and held his attention, the way they bounced, the bronze skin topped by dusky nipples that practically begged for his mouth. He leaned forward to answer that silent plea, but she maneuvered out of the way. "Nope."

Motherfucker. He was beginning to feel like a conveniently warm blow-up doll. "If you're not going to let me touch you, what the hell are you here for?"

"This." She reached behind her with one hand and cupped his balls, squeezing lightly. The pressure nearly sent him to the moon. It was only made worse by the way she shuddered, her eyes closed and pure bliss on her face.

She squeezed him one more time, and he lost it, moving his hips as much as he could, pumping into her as his orgasm rocked through him. He had to close his eyes from the sheer intensity of it, though he opened them again almost immediately. He didn't want to miss a second of this.

Regan kneaded his shoulders, a little laugh escaping. "That was fun."

Fun? *Fun?* Brock shook his head and blinked a few times. As soon as he could move his legs again, he was going to show her exactly who had control of this situation.

After a long moment, she straightened and climbed off him. He tried not to be moved by the perfection of her body, but he was only human and he'd bet she spent a lot of time working for it. She turned around to grab her skirt and shirt, her rounded ass making him want to take a bite. Yeah, this was a woman familiar with Spin class.

Then he registered the fact that she was getting dressed. "What are you doing?"

"What's it look like?" She fastened her bra and shrugged into her shirt. With every button, he lost sight of more skin— and his chance of turning the night around. She picked up her panties, seemed to consider, and dropped them on the bed. "I'm all for cherishing the memories."

She started for the door and he lunged, grabbing her wrist. "Stay."

"What?"

"You heard me. Stay with me tonight." The sex had been hot as hell, but he wasn't even close to getting her out of his system.

She bit her lip, looking indecisive for the first time since he'd met her. He pulled her a step closer, and then another. "I want to taste you."

He realized his mistake as soon as she tensed, but it was too late to take the words back. She jerked her hand out of his. "Thanks, but no thanks." She arched an eyebrow, once again the untouchable Regan. "Enjoy the afterglow, Scarlett. And just think, you didn't even have to work for it."

Holy shit. She was going to just walk out and leave him sitting there with his pants around his ankles? Brock glared. "You sure know how to make a guy feel special."

Her flinch was almost imperceptible, but it was more than enough to make him feel like an ass. He made an effort to brush it away. She'd come in here, ordered him down, and fucked him, and hell if it hadn't been one of the hottest experiences of his life. He didn't like realizing that, and he sure as fuck wasn't going to tell *her*, but it was hotter than he would have guessed, being used for a beautiful woman's pleasure. "Regan—"

"Let's be honest here, okay? You just came harder than you thought possible—and my orgasm was pretty cool, too. So thanks, Brock. I had a good time, and I know you did, too. Have a nice life." Then she turned around and strode out the door, her shoes dangling from one hand.

He sat there in silence for a few minutes, still trying to process what the hell just happened. With a sigh, he pushed to his feet, his muscles shaking. He didn't like that she thought he was so worthless that she could just come in here and use him as a giant sex toy. Yeah, it'd been hot, but there was a level of dirty feeling he wasn't prepared to deal with. It might have been different if their relationship was any less antagonistic, but he was reasonably sure she didn't think much of him. Right now he wasn't too fond of her, either.

Brock thought back over what just happened, to her flinch when he'd snapped at her. He'd hurt her. If he could do that with a few careless words, she wasn't carting around nearly as thick a skin as she pretended. As he turned on the shower, he muttered, "Don't go there. Woman is nothing but trouble, and you damn well know it."

That didn't stop his curiosity from perking up and taking notice. He wanted to know more about Regan and what made her tick. If he could get under her skin and clothes in the process... Well, he was okay with that, too.

• • •

Regan didn't breathe easy until she was back in her room with the door shut safely behind her. All she could picture was the look on Brock's face right before she left the room, the anger and determination blatant across his features.

He thought this was just the opening match.

No way. They'd had their fun, as two consenting adults did from time to time, and now it was over. She had no place in her life for a too-sexy-for-her-good country boy who liked to cruise through life on his daddy's coattails. The McNeills were known in Tennessee for buying up all the mom-and-pop stores and streamlining the businesses while still "preserving the cultural flavor" or some shit, and their name had been popping up more and more as time went on. Brock hadn't had to work for the lifestyle he had. She'd bet he hadn't gone hungry once in his life.

She glanced at her computer, and actually took a step toward it before she caught herself. No. There was no reason to do research on Brock. She was done with him, and he wouldn't know what to do with her even if he caught her. Honestly, judging by the comments she overheard him making to Reed—something about the ass on the bartender and then, in the next breath, about the *set* on one of the other wedding guests—he was a player with a capital *P*.

And she wasn't interested in being a notch on someone's bedpost unless it was on *her* terms.

Satisfied she was well and truly done with Brock, she crossed to her computer for an entirely different reason. Logan, the best man.

He was everything she was supposed to want—brilliant and cultured and driven. The kind of man who fit right into her life plan. Her friends might laugh at how rigid said plan was, but it had been the thing to keep her in line in college, and keeping to her plan was what made her as successful at her job as she'd been. She had her eye on the prize, and she didn't let anything get in the way of obtaining it.

Her parents had given up a hell of a lot to get her into college and make sure she graduated without the plague of debt so many of her alumni suffered from. It gave her the freedom to make slightly riskier career choices—which had all paid off. She wouldn't be where she was if it wasn't for her parents, and she owed it to them not to throw it all away.

Which is where her plan came in.

Married to a corporate man by thirty. At twenty-seven, her options were slowly starting to dwindle. And her friends were moving on with their lives. Kady was the first to actually settle down, but the other women were sure to follow.

But that was neither here nor there. She had her plan, and her plan wasn't going to be altered just because she was suddenly starting to feel lonely. Maybe the right guy would walk into her life and change all that.

The right guy could very well be Logan McCade.

She typed his name into her search engine and cruised

through the results, determined to take more than the five minutes she'd managed before she got on the plane from NYC. Most of them concerned his company, Defy Gravity, and its many successes. Nice. He got his MBA at Yale, and had been doing well for himself ever since, conquering one barrier after another and making his company a raging success. Honestly, he was borderline disgustingly perfect.

What could it hurt to get to know him a little more? She couldn't have drawn up a man who fit her plan better if she'd tried.

Against her better judgment, her thoughts slid back to the man she'd just left, bringing up a side-by-side image of him and Logan. Damn it. What did it matter if Brock was the one who made her toes curl? He was the love 'em and leave 'em weeping and clutching their skirts type.

They'd had their fun and now it was over.

Then again, what could one more little Google search hurt? And if she called in a favor with Addison... It was totally justified. She *had* just slept with the man, so there was nothing wrong with finding out a little more about him. Addison had all the best connections for finding out everything regarding new clients before she took them on. Regan had never figured out how she found all the dirt on people so quickly, but Addison was a mother hen when it came to her clients. She refused to take on someone she wouldn't be able to back 100 percent. It was part of the reason they got along so well—Regan understood and respected the kind of drive and dedication it took to be a success.

Her fingers flew over the keyboard before she could talk herself out of it. Brock McNeill, younger son of Vince

McNeill, owner of the biggest corporation south of Kentucky. His oldest son, Caine, currently held the CEO position, and Brock was listed as the VP.

Shockingly, the information hadn't changed since the last time she did this search. Further down the page there was a link to a prominent gossip column. Regan rolled her eyes. An art gallery opening—just the place rich men liked to show up with gorgeous women on their arms and pretend they knew what the hell they were looking at. As expected, when she pulled up the article, there was a picture of Brock and a woman whose chest sure as hell wasn't the one she was born with. She leaned against him, smiling up as if he were the most interesting person she'd ever met.

Having been on the receiving end of his charm, Regan couldn't blame her. Even knowing better, she had still wanted to bask in his presence. Thank God she was far too stubborn for any of that nonsense.

The article went on to detail the women Brock had been seen with and project who might be on his arm next. Hmmm. She closed out of it and went down the list, but each link was more of the same. There was next to no information on what Brock did at McNeill Enterprises, other than listing him as the VP. Which meant she was right—for all intents and purposes, he held a figurehead position.

Shocking.

With a laugh, she closed the laptop. She'd pegged him right. He was rudderless, and he didn't show any signs of changing that any time soon. Still…

"Damn it." She grabbed her phone and swiped through her contacts.

It rang only once before a cheerful female voice answered.

"Regan! I haven't heard from you in ages."

"I know. I'm sorry. I've been so busy trying to convince this software designer that he'd be happier in New York that I haven't actually seen my city in two weeks."

Addison laughed. "You poor thing, getting to travel all the time."

"I seem to recall you telling me that it would take a crowbar and half a ton of dynamite to get you out of New York." Her appreciation of the city was one of the things they'd bonded over when they first met.

"What can I say? I love it here, and I don't have time to leave even if I wanted to. Speaking of which… Aren't you in the middle of nowhere for your sorority sister's wedding? Why are you calling me? I suppose it's too much to hope for that some cowboy has swept you off your feet and you're announcing your engagement?"

The image of Brock shirtless in that chair seemed determined to imprint itself on her brain. He was no cowboy—and he wasn't engagement material—but he'd definitely made an impression. "Nothing like that. I need some information."

"Right now? You're supposed to be on vacation and having a little fun."

A shiver rolled through her as she remembered the feeling of Brock inside her. Damn. Even the memory was enough to make her want to crawl back in his lap for a second go-round. "Trust me, I'm playing plenty while I'm here."

"I expect the dirty details when you get back."

"You know, if you played a little more, you wouldn't have to live vicariously through me." It was the same thing she'd said countless times before.

As expected, Addison gave her the same response. "I don't need to play. I'm happiest when I'm making other people happy. But stop trying to change the subject. Who's the lucky person you need info on?"

Logan. But when she opened her mouth, it was a different name that came out. "Brock McNeill."

"The usual?"

"Yeah, I need to know all his dirty little secrets." Though she was sure that list would be longer than her arm. God, why had she bothered listing him at all? He wasn't the one she wanted. Regan bit her lip, hating the way her heart sped up at the thought of him. Wrong. It was so wrong. "And I need the same on Logan McCade."

"Will do. I don't suppose this is for pleasure instead of business?"

"It might be."

"Holy crap, has Regan Wakefield finally found a man who's making her think of settling down?"

"I won't know until I get more information, now will I? And Addison, thanks."

"Anytime. You know that."

"Talk to you soon." She hung up and dropped her phone onto the desk. What the hell was wrong with her? She shouldn't be spending any of her time and resources on Brock, no matter how much she'd enjoyed the sex.

Finding out more about Logan was the goal.

She frowned at her complete lack of excitement over the thought. It must be because she hadn't really had a chance to talk to him. Once she did, things would click into place.

Regan picked up the helpfully detailed itinerary she

had no doubt Julie was responsible for. Tomorrow was the scavenger hunt. The perfect opportunity for getting close to Logan and figuring out if they had spark potential.

Plan firmly in place, she headed for the shower—no way could she sleep with the scent of Brock on her skin. It made her body feel hot and achy, wondering what it would have been like to let him actually get his hands on her. She shook her head. It didn't matter how good he made her feel, he wasn't the settling-down type, and that's what she wanted now that thirty was on the horizon.

Why was she even thinking about this? He'd had his taste, and now he'd move on to greener pastures. And it seemed like he'd done this kind of thing enough that she could be sure things wouldn't be awkward while she did the same. Just in case, though, she'd avoid him as much as possible for the rest of the week.

No need to overcomplicate things.

Chapter Four

Regan should have known she'd run into Julie at the gym at such an ungodly hour in the morning. Her best friend had always been something of an overachiever, though she'd balanced it out with a wicked wild streak in college. After her sister died, though, the wild child disappeared, replaced by an almost manic need to please everyone she came in contact with. Regan kept hoping she'd snap out of it, but grief could be a strange emotion.

Immediately, she could tell something was up with Julie, though apparently it wasn't anger at Regan for switching room keys on her. Which meant she'd had a brilliantly good time with Mr. Tall, Dark, and Dangerous the night of the bachelorette party. But the way Julie was sprinting on that treadmill meant that either things had taken a turn for the worst…or they were going too well. She raised her eyebrows. "Uh-oh. She's madder than a wet hen."

"Now who's going Southern?"

Was what she'd done with Brock written on her forehead? "Correction. I've *gone* Southern." Images from last night flashed through head, the sight of his cock sliding in and out of her, every muscle in his body standing out as he fought not to touch her… The look of rage on his face when she walked out on him. Ugh. She pushed it away, wishing she could push away the uncomfortable feeling twisting her stomach as easily. It was over and done with. "Now I'm going West. It's like my own version of the Gold Rush."

Somehow Julie managed to keep a straight face. "Panning for orgasms."

"I couldn't have put it better myself." Though she had no idea how anything with Logan could live up to last night. Not when Brock managed to do with one look what most men could do with an hour of good, hard work.

She really needed to stop thinking about him. "I need a… What are those things called? The scrubby ones made out of metal?"

"Sweet baby Jesus, Regan. Steel wool? How have you managed to survive as long as you have without it?"

"You already know the answer to that." She laughed. "I don't clean. Not when I can help it."

"Isn't that the truth? I still remember the life forms that your leftovers created in our fridge while we were gone on spring break during… What year was it? Sophomore?"

"Junior. We made the pledges clean it." It had been a simpler time in a lot of ways, though her stress level had been through the roof. "It wasn't my fault! It was in the middle of midterms and that old witch Cliver gave us two papers to write on top of it. I don't think I slept for a week."

"No one was sleeping after they got a look at the fridge.

It was scarier than a snowstorm in the middle of July." Julie glanced at the clock on the wall across from them. "I have to go. I'm late!"

"You're late, you're late, for a very important date… With Mr. Tall, Dark, and Dangerous?"

She slammed the stop button. "That's over and done with. Deader than a doornail. I have to clean up after last night's party."

"You know, I think there's someone who does that for a living. Oh wait, I know what they're called—housekeepers. Why don't you slow down, let someone else carry the burden, and actually enjoy yourself?"

Julie gave her a look like she was crazy. "I *am* enjoying myself. Taking care of people makes me happy."

Yeah, but who's going to take care of you? Regan didn't say it, because she knew Julie would just laugh her off. But she watched her best friend rush out of the gym, and she worried.

She kept running for a while after Julie left, her thoughts circling totally unhelpfully. It was only around mile four that things started to fall into place. The scavenger hunt would be pairs of people searching for whatever the hell Kady had come up with on the list. So she'd dress to kill and work at catching Logan's eye for a little alone time. From there, it'd be cake.

If there was one thing Regan knew how to do, it was sway a man into seeing things her way. And right now, her way included Logan and a date.

She slowed to a walk and then stopped altogether. After wiping the sweat off her face, she headed out. A shower and a full-on primp was on the books, so she'd need all the time she could spare.

When the elevator opened on the floor below hers, she almost cursed aloud—she wasn't the vainest creature on this planet, but if you walked out of the gym looking pretty, you were wasting your time there. She hadn't planned on giving anyone a good look at her sweaty self.

Obviously she should have taken the stairs.

Then Logan stepped into the elevator and she wanted to curse even more. This was *not* the impression she'd planned on making when she said she was going to catch his eye. Frustrated, she pasted a smile on her face. "Logan. Fancy meeting you here."

He frowned for half a second, as if he didn't recognize her. Then his hazel eyes widened. "Regan. Nice to see you. Going down?"

Only last night on Brock. She looked away, wishing she could banish memories of him as quickly as they popped into her head. "Nope. Up." She took in his rumpled clothing— the same clothing he'd been wearing last night. "You look like you've been getting into some trouble."

"Nothing like that." His smile was nice, though she couldn't help comparing it to a certain Southern boy's. "I was up late working."

Well, hell. She had to admire a man who had that kind of commitment to his business. Working late nights was the name of the game for most of her week—the Chinese takeout down the street from her apartment knew her by name and order before she even opened her mouth.

What had Logan been working on? She started to ask, but the elevator dinged again, opening on her floor. "This is my stop."

"It was nice talking to you."

She backed through the doors. "Maybe we can talk more during the scavenger hunt."

"That'd be great."

As the doors shut, she sagged against the wall. So much for leaving him wanting more. She should have taken off her tank top before she left the gym so she didn't look like something an alley cat dragged in. Then at least he would have been distracted with all the skin she'd have been showing and ignored the rest of her. Even as she considered it, she wondered what the hell she was stressing about? As she walked into her room, Regan yanked out her ponytail holder with more force than strictly necessary.

She wasn't a precious little princess who dressed up so men would tell her she was pretty and fall at her feet. She wore the clothing she did for *her*, and because it was just another kind of armor. Like it or not, people judged her on the way she dressed, and failing to look professional could cost her a client.

If seeing her in some sweaty gym clothes was enough to make Logan blow her off, then he was an idiot.

Still… No reason to give him another reason to think twice.

She dug through her suitcase, coming up with a dress she'd bought a few weeks ago that hugged every curve. The texturing changed it from skanky to sexy, but it didn't leave a whole lot to the imagination. Combine it with a killer pair of heels and Logan would have to be dead not to sit up and take notice of her.

• • •

Running into Reed didn't do a damn bit for Brock's mood. He'd wanted some time alone to stew about what happened last night, to finally put it out of his head. It had been obvious when he saw his friend leaning against the side of the building that he had something on his mind. They weren't the types to pour out their hearts, but a man wore a certain look on his face when dealing with woman problems.

Low and behold, he'd been as snarly as Brock had ever seen him. "Told you she was trouble."

Yeah, he had. And Brock had ignored the underlying advice to steer clear of her before, and he was going to keep doing it. "Trouble is a significant underestimation."

Reed glanced at him in surprise. "Did you swallow a dictionary last night?"

Christ. "I can use words longer than one syllable when I put my mind to it. When did everyone start thinking the opposite?"

"You mean, when did you start giving a shit?"

"That, too."

Reed shrugged. "Maybe it's the altitude."

"Altitude indeed." He wished he could blame last night on something so simple, but it'd be a dirty lie. He'd been on the losing side as soon as he followed Regan out of the bar. "Any man with half a brain would give that woman and her fool heels a wide berth."

"I've never known you to shy away from a challenge. Hell, you jumped off that cliff at the rock quarry when we were thirteen even when Colton refused to."

"This isn't a challenge. This is impossible."

Reed snorted. "Is that really going to be enough to stop you?"

Of course he'd say that. Growing up, he'd always been the reckless one, the one who made the questionable choices and the first to jump into any situation. Through it all, Brock had been hot on his heels. Reed and Colton were a staple of his childhood, the two kids who had never expected him to magically transform into a clone of his older brother. Every time he'd had a blowup with his parents, they'd been there to take his mind off things.

And Reed…he had his own cross to bear. Even if Brock had been in danger of forgetting that, all it would take was a quick step to that hot night when they were twelve, and he had sneaked out to recruit Reed for some prank or other. What he'd seen when he got to Reed's house had changed the course of his entire life.

Brock rubbed a hand over his face. He'd never told Reed about the company he formed five years ago—or why—and today wasn't going to be the day he came clean. Today was about figuring out what the hell he was going to do about Regan. "She's a damned force of nature."

"And you're not?"

"Well, hell, when you put it that way."

"You're just looking for a reason to chase her. You don't need one. Get chasing."

Brock grinned, thinking back to Regan's dog reference last night. "Wuff."

"That's more like it."

He glanced at his watch. "It's getting to be that time." As much as he wasn't looking forward to the scavenger hunt, he wouldn't miss the chance to see little miss city girl wandering around in the woods. Anything that put that woman off her game was a good thing in his book.

"Go on ahead. I don't need a babysitter."

He never had. Reed might have made some fucked-up choices a few years ago, but it was the wake-up call he'd needed to get his life together. He still wasn't the poster boy for well-adjusted, but Reed had been there for him over the years, even if they hadn't talked about the reason Brock needed someone to lean on. Colton was gone nine months out of twelve, and while he made their summers full of good times, it was out of sight, out of mind when they were kids. But Reed never left. He was always willing to sneak out and walk aimlessly around town when Brock was feeling trapped by his father's demands, or to come up with some crazy thing to keep them both distracted from the homes they had to go back to.

Brock *knew* he was lucky to be born into the family he was, but he constantly felt strangled by his father's expectations. Weighed down by the fact that he'd never be Caine. His older brother did everything right, and no matter how hard he tried, he never measured up.

So he'd stopped trying.

Shit, he hadn't meant to take that little trip down memory lane. Brock decided to take the long way through the grounds to where they were supposed to meet for the scavenger hunt. He needed time to get his game face on, because he had to figure out what the fuck he was going to do about Regan.

Why should he do anything at all? She'd had her fun, and she couldn't be clearer about not wanting anything to do with him again. Why not stop kicking a dead horse? It would sure as hell make his life a lot simpler.

He rounded the corner to find a group of women

gathered. There was the pretty blond cheerleader type who'd caught Reed's eye, the quiet redhead, Kady with her almost-bride glow...and Regan.

He let himself look his fill, taking in the waves in her hair that had to have taken some serious time to create, the dress that hugged every curve and made him wonder if she were wearing panties underneath, and those damned heels. He'd never cared one way or another for the shit women wore on their feet, but something about her bright-red heels made him picture how she'd look in nothing but them.

Kady said something and Regan shot a panicked look his way. He took the opportunity to grin at her. If anything, she seemed even less pleased. Good. At least he wasn't the only one uncomfortable here.

As the group dispersed, the little redhead wandered over. She had the distracted look of someone with something serious on her mind. "Hey, Irish, a penny for your thoughts."

The redhead, Christine, he thought her name was, made a face. "As if I haven't heard *that* one before."

"What can I say, I'm a traditionalist."

She snorted. "I doubt it."

She was really cute in a girl-next-door way. The kind of woman a man settled down and had a boatload of kids with. The kind of woman he normally avoided like the plague—he wasn't the type to leave a trail of broken hearts behind him, and women like this didn't have sex without complications. Brock wasn't a settling-down type. Maybe in the future, but right now it wasn't in the cards. He had too much to accomplish before he went down that road.

Still, he gave her his most charming smile. It would be smarter to focus on Christine than to spend his time in this borderline obsession with a certain high-strung brunette. "Maybe you should give me a chance to prove it."

Christine's eyes went wide and a laugh erupted from her lips. She slapped a hand over her mouth. "Oh my God, Regan was right. You really are incorrigible."

He sighed. "You Tri Delts are bad for a man's ego."

"Sorry." She glanced sideways, her mouth tightening at whatever it was she saw. Before he could follow her gaze, she'd turned those blue eyes back on him. "If it helps, you're really good-looking. But I'll bet you've had plenty of women tell you that, haven't you?"

"A gentleman never tells." A flash of movement caught his attention. Regan stood next to Kady, glaring daggers. She snatched a piece of paper out of her friend's hands, and she stalked over to him. It wasn't every day he saw a woman who walked in six-inch heels like they were flats, but Regan made it look effortless.

And he really needed to stop obsessing over her fucking shoes.

She shoved a paper at his chest. "Howdy, partner." Then she turned a genuinely sweet smile at Christine. "Sorry, honey, but I'm doing you a favor. You don't want to spend any more time with this asshat than strictly necessary."

Christine's gaze jumped between them and then away. "Better than the alternative," she muttered. With a pained sigh, she walked away, leaving him to Regan's tender mercies.

She barely waited for her friend to get out of earshot before she spun on him. "You stay away from her."

"Why? I think she's a sweetheart."

She glared. "She's a nice girl, and you'd eat her alive. Then I'd take a truly scary amount of pleasure in killing you and throwing your body in a Dumpster."

Even though it was aimed at him, her protectiveness of her friend chipped away at some of the anger he felt over how last night had ended. Some of it. "Aw, you're adorable. I reckon you've never seen woods before right now."

She flipped her hair over her shoulder, but there was a twinkle in her eyes. "Scarlett, please. I was a Girl Scout."

That startled a laugh out of him. "And pray tell, why did you drop out?"

"Do you know what's in the woods? Bugs. Things that make freaky noises. Squirrels who are only too happy to go for your throat." She shuddered. "I'm more cut out for the concrete jungle." Then she seemed to realize they were having an actual conversation without animosity, because her eyes narrowed. "But that changes nothing. Stay away from Christine. She's not like us. You'd hurt her."

The unspoken comment being that he couldn't hurt Regan. Since he didn't *want* to hurt her, that was great news. Or it would be if it didn't signify the fact that she'd never care enough about him for him to be able to hurt her. He shouldn't care. She was just some chick at one of his friends' weddings.

Damn it, he *did* care.

"You should let me take you out sometime." The words were out before he realized he was going to say it.

The shocked look on her face was almost funny. Almost. "Hitting the moonshine a little early today, don't you think?"

"Enough with the country boy references." He'd bet she'd never touched moonshine.

"I just call it like I see it." She crossed her arms under her chest, and he did his damnedest not to stare at her breasts.

"Look, I had a great time last night and all, but this just isn't going to work out like you want it to."

She thought she had him all figured out. It shouldn't surprise him. Everyone else did, too. "Why not, Regan? How the hell do you know what I want from this? I don't remember you sticking around long enough to talk last night. "

"There is no 'this.'" She motioned between them. "You aren't the kind of guy who settles down. There's nothing wrong with that, but I'm not looking to waste my time. To be frank, Logan is more my speed."

He stared. Was she for real? "Logan."

"Yeah. He's cultured, has excellent taste, and owns his own business. He's not the type to flit from woman to woman."

"Have you exchanged more than two words with the guy?" Brock had. When they'd all gone out for drinks the first night here, he'd had a chance to talk to Logan for a little while. He was a decent guy. A little work-obsessed for Brock's taste—and a whole lot too much like his brother Caine.

Right now he kind of wished Logan was an ass so he could hate the man.

She shrugged one shoulder. "We've talked."

Of course they had. How could Logan not lose his head over Regan? She was all glitter and fireworks that drew the gaze—though he'd bet she hadn't shown *Logan* her claws.

She glanced sideways and her eyes widened. "Quick, say something funny."

The change in subject almost gave him whiplash. "What?"

Regan gritted her teeth. "A joke. Tell a joke, or something."

"What the hell are you talking about?"

"Good Lord, you're hopeless." She leaned in, so close he got a whiff of her perfume, and laid her hand on his arm. Then she threw her head back and let loose the most carefree and intoxicating laugh he'd ever heard in his life. It hit him like a lightning bolt, a shock that he wasn't prepared for.

The shock turned sour as soon as he realized what she'd caught sight of. A man had just walked past their group, shooting an interested look in her direction. Brock shook his head, realizing she'd mistaken the stranger for Logan. "Stand down, Mrs. McCade. That is not the man you're looking for."

"Shit." Her smile looked a little strained around the edges. "Nice *Star Wars* reference, even if you butchered the delivery."

He never would have pegged her for a *Star Wars* fan, but he refused to pursue that curiosity because there were bigger issues at hand. "You were going to use me to get his attention."

"Was I?"

Yes, damn it. That's exactly what she'd been doing. "What's the pretty boy have that I don't?"

"Don't you think that's the pot calling the kettle black?" She waved her hand at his face. "And, like I said before, he's charming, successful, and has a fantastic career."

"Darlin', I'm VP of McNeill Enterprises."

She laughed. "Oh please. You're a *figurehead*. What kind of skill set do you bring to the table? The ability to charm women out of their panties?"

He didn't let himself react, but only because he'd heard

the same argument more times than he wanted to count. *Why can't you just settle down like Caine? Caine never would have let that client walk away. Caine brings more to this company than you ever will. Caine is the future.*

It made it really hard for him not to hate his brother when he was constantly being measured against him—and coming up short. "I have skills."

"I'm sure you do, but I'm equally sure that I wouldn't hire you."

Brock looked around, taking in the fact that they were now alone. "That's a damn shame, because it looks like you're stuck with me."

Chapter Five

Regan fought back a curse. She'd planned on making her way over to Logan once she'd gotten his attention by showing him just how good a time she was having with Brock. It was a good plan…but Logan was apparently a no-show, and she hadn't been in the right mind since she'd seen Brock aiming that goddamn panty-dropper smile of his at Christine. Her friend was smart and normally she'd have no trouble telling him where to stuff it, but with all the new changes in her life, Regan was afraid she was too vulnerable to handle a man like Brock.

That was the *only* reason she'd practically run over there. Because she was a good friend. Not because the thought of Brock and Christine sneaking off together made her physically sick to her stomach.

Now she was stuck with him. *Shit*.

She glanced over the list. Where the hell had Kady come up with this crap? A freaking feather? With a few exceptions—a newspaper—all of it required her to go into the forest surrounding Beaver Creek Resort. "On second thought, I'm not that interested in seeing whatever Kady came up with for a prize. You go on ahead and try your luck."

"Aw, come on. I wouldn't expect you to back off so easily."

"I don't back down, and I don't lose when I set my mind on something." But there was nothing wrong with a tactful retreat.

"Obviously you don't want Logan as much as you think if you're already giving up. In case you didn't know, that guy lives for this nature shit. He's probably already out here gathering ancient Indian arrowheads and fossils and fuck-all if I know."

Giving up. Two dirty words if she ever heard them. She didn't give up. Never had. No, Regan analyzed the problem, and then proceeded to find her way over, under, around, or—sometimes—through it.

She'd let her reluctance to spend any more time than necessary with Brock cloud her judgment. He was right—if she wanted a chance at Logan, she was going to have to work a little harder. Which meant going into that treed hellhole.

Maybe she should have packed some bug spray.

"Fine. Let's go. But keep your goddamn hands to yourself."

"Me?" He grabbed the paper. "I'm a gentleman. You're the one who practically threw a bag over my head and dragged me off to be your love slave."

"It has nothing to do with love." And now she couldn't get the image of his sliding in and out of her as she rode him out of her mind. She gritted her teeth. Fucking fabulous.

"My mistake." He made a showy gesture, waving her toward the path. "Ladies first—even ones with dubious virtue."

"Dubious. You've been using that Word of the Day app again." She strode into the trees, taking half a second to wish she'd worn more practical shoes. The problem was she didn't *own* any practical shoes aside from her gym shoes. And she wouldn't be caught dead in them outside of a treadmill. "Too much more of that and someone who didn't know better might think you actually have an IQ to brag about."

"Careful—I might think you like me if you keep up that kind of talk."

"God forbid." It was darker beneath the trees, the tall trunks cutting off the sun and creating shadows. Something moved off to her right and she jumped. "What the hell was that?"

Brock followed her gaze. "Ah, yes. The rabid tree squirrel. Very dangerous." He turned back with a grin that made her stomach flip-flop. "Don't worry—I'll protect you."

When had anyone ever offered her something like that, even jokingly?

She knew the answer without even thinking about it. Never. She was Regan, independent lover, corporate warrior, driven career woman. People looked to *her* for answers and to take care of their needs. They never offered to return the favor.

He's making fun of you, you idiot. Get your shit together. She swallowed down the unfamiliar feeling in her throat and forced a cocky smile. "Squirrel vanquisher. I'd be sure to add that to your résumé."

Satisfied she had the last laugh, she turned and started

walking again. A feather. How freaking hard was it to find a feather in the forest? Shouldn't there be birds flapping around and being annoying? She didn't see a single sign of one.

"Don't forget to mention my orgasm-bringing skills." His voice came from entirely too close behind her. "I mean, hell, I didn't even touch you and you came within seconds. Imagine what I could do if I actually got my mouth on you."

She jumped and then cursed herself for showing even that much response. Making sure her smile was in place, she turned—and jumped again. He stood not a foot from her, towering over her despite her six-inch heels. This close, his magnetism was an almost-physical thing. She had to actively concentrate on not leaning into him.

Frankly, it pissed her off.

So she cocked her hip out and propped her hand on it. "I think your memory is faulty. If you think back *really hard*, it'll become clear that I brought about my own orgasms. You just happened to be there."

If she expected him to jerk back or look horrified or hurt, she was sadly mistaken. His grin never wavered. "Is that so?"

God, this man's voice should be illegal. When he looked at her like that, it made it really hard to remember why touching him was a terrible idea. She lifted her chin. "Yep."

"It's adorable the way you have to work yourself into a tizzy to keep from kissing me."

"*A tizzy?*"

"Mm-hmm." Had he moved closer? She wasn't sure. But then his grin widened and she lost her thought. Goddamn laugh lines. "An adorable tizzy. All quick talking and the like, as if it really means anything."

"It does." She licked her lips. "It means I'm not even remotely interested in you."

"Not even a little bit, huh?" His hands dropped to her waist, and even though she knew she should shove him off, she couldn't help following his gentle nudging forward. Brock's gaze fastened on her mouth. "I'm about to make a liar out of you."

"Wha—"

He took her mouth like he was sure of his welcome, like he knew it was exactly what she wanted. And it was better than she could have imagined. Brock's tongue dipped between her lips to caress hers, the taste of him intoxicating. She slipped her arms around his neck and ran her fingers through his too-long hair. The man was temptation personified. It just wasn't fair.

She moaned as he moved over her jaw and down her throat, his whiskers rasping against her skin. He nipped the spot where her neck met her shoulder and then continued down. When she realized his intention she arched her back, trying to give him better access. God help her, but this was what she'd wanted from the moment she'd set eyes on him earlier, the swagger in his stride speaking of the breathtakingly sexy things they'd done last night.

"Jump."

His meaning became clear when he grabbed her ass and slid his hands down the back of her thighs. Regan hopped and wrapped her legs around his waist, the move making her dress ride up to indecent levels. Anyone who walked up this path would get the show of their lives.

She shook her head, trying to think past the lust muddling

her brain. "Someone could see…"

He nodded and stepped off the path, winding through the trees until they couldn't see it anymore. She had a panicked realization that she was in the freaking forest. Then he kissed her again, and Regan decided Brock would just have to live up to his squirrel-vanquishing abilities because she wasn't sure she was capable of walking away from him right now.

While she was freaking out about being surrounded by nature, he'd taken advantage of her distraction to slip her dress strap off her shoulder. One good tug and he freed her breast. "Jesus, woman. I *knew* you weren't wearing a bra."

"I—" She gasped when he took her nipple into his mouth. "Don't stop doing that."

He cupped her ass, shifting her until the hard ridge of him pressed right where she needed it. Using little motions, he made her ride him—something she was only too happy to help with. Noises came out of her mouth that didn't sound remotely human, but she couldn't help it, not when the pressure built inside her, pushed ever higher by the slide of her silk panties against his slacks and his mouth on her nipple.

"More. Oh my God, more."

He released her breast and reclaimed her mouth as he circled his hips, the new sensation sending her flying over the edge. She clung to him as she came, shudders racking her body that he seemed to take pleasure in drawing out. Only when he'd wrung every bit from her body did he help her stand and step back.

Regan stared at him, using every bit of strength she had not to let her shaking legs collapse. He was breathing just as hard as she was, and there was no mistaking the length of his cock making a rather impressive imprint on his slacks.

While she was staring at his hips, he caught her chin in unyielding fingers and forced her to meet his eyes. "Let's not tell lies between friends. You just came so fucking hard, you can barely stand right now. That wasn't you using my body— that was *me* making you lose your damn mind."

"I—"

But he continued right over her. "So if I'm such a fuckup, what does that make you—the woman who can't keep her hands off me?"

Before she could come up with an answer, he turned and strode away, leaving her alone, surrounded by trees. She wrapped her arms around herself, trying to dredge up some anger. It was slow in coming, battling through the desire still sparking along her skin. So much for squirrel vanquisher. He'd lured her out here, made her orgasm, and left her to whatever bloodthirsty creature found her first.

"Lured? Really?" Okay, so that wasn't strictly accurate. It was hard to lure someone anywhere when they're wrapped around you like a deranged spider monkey.

She gave herself a shake. This wasn't about him abandoning her to die. No, this was about him throwing down a gauntlet. He thought he could put her in her place? Fat chance.

She had bigger fish to fry.

But if it made Brock feel better to think he'd one-upped her this time, he could just go on thinking that. And she'd do her damnedest not to dwell on the fact that he'd just given her one of the best orgasms of her life.

She straightened her dress and turned a slow circle. He'd

only taken like five steps to get back here. It shouldn't be this hard to figure out which way he'd gone. Regan turned around again. Or it wouldn't be hard if she were an expert tracker-slash-zombie-killer like Daryl from *The Walking Dead*.

Which way was the path? She turned a slow circle, trying to figure out where Brock had gone. All she had to do was take that first step, pick a direction and walk. It was easy. It wasn't like she was in the wilds of upper New York State.

Oh my God, I'm going to wander for hours and end up dying ten feet from safety because that asshole left me here.

"Lord, woman, the path is right here." Brock stalked back through the trees, and she had to clasp her hands behind her back to keep from throwing herself at him and begging him not to leave her out here alone again. He stopped a few feet away and narrowed his eyes. "Are you okay?"

Not even a little bit. She couldn't tell if her hands were shaking so hard that they were making her shoulders shake or if that was her entire body struggling not to cling to the safety Brock suddenly represented. "Sure. Why wouldn't I be okay? It's not like I can't Google Maps my way to safety."

She *knew* her fear of the forest was unnatural; she still couldn't stop her body's shaking. She had to get out of here right now, or she was in serious danger of bawling in front of Brock.

Over her dead body.

Chapter Six

Brock stepped closer to Regan, moving slowly so as not to spook her further. Because she was spooked. Her eyes were a little too wide and her entire body was shaking so hard he could see it from here. "Sweetheart, it's okay. I'm here."

If he'd stopped to think before storming off to make his point, he would have realized there was a reason she hated the woods beyond her being a city girl. City girls turned up their noses at places like this, but they didn't jump at little noises or panic at the thought of moving off the path.

Stupid of him to miss that.

He touched her shoulders, giving her the chance to move away, but she only took half a step closer. "You left me out here."

So fucking stupid. "I'm sorry."

"I didn't know which way to go and—" She snapped her mouth close and took a shuddering breath. "I'm fine."

She was a hell of a long ways off fine, but now wasn't

the time to point it out. "Why don't we get you back to civilization?"

"God, yes."

He slipped his arm around her shoulders, ready to catch her if she stumbled in those ridiculous heels, and guided her back to the path. She didn't relax until they left the trees completely, her shaking lessening and then disappearing altogether. She took her next few steps a bit quicker, moving out from beneath his arm. "I'm okay."

Did she realize how many times she'd said it? He didn't think so. A woman like her wasn't going to respond well to coddling, but he also couldn't leave her alone when she was in such an obviously fragile state of mind. Truth was he didn't want to leave her just yet. So he went with the most blunt approach. "What do you need?"

Regan blinked, seeming to come back to herself a little. "To sweat until I feel in control again."

It was on the tip of his tongue to suggest one particular activity that would fit the bill, but he couldn't do it. Brock might want to get inside her again more than was healthy for his state of mind, but he wasn't the type of man to take advantage of a woman so clearly off her game. So he put a check on his dick and went with a safer question. "Do you run? Or are you one of those prissy-pants elliptical users?"

Her eyes flashed. "I can run you into the ground, Scarlett."

There was the spitfire he knew and enjoyed. He grinned. "Prove it."

"Gym. Fifteen minutes."

"Done." He watched her walk away, glad to see some of the swing back in her step. Shaking his head, he headed to his room, happy for the excuse to change out of these damn clothes. But he'd been informed by both Colton and Kady that they expected him to dress like a grown-up, not in the faded jeans and T-shirts he favored, for the duration of the week. It was a relief to throw on some basketball shorts and one of his favorite old T-shirts, and head to the gym.

He found Regan already there, dressed in a pair of those tiny black shorts that were designed to bring a man to his knees, and a tank top. She nodded briefly at him. "Let's do this."

"So serious. You really need to learn to loosen up."

As expected, she bristled. "And you could stand to loosen up a whole lot less." She hesitated, some of that vulnerability showing on her face. "Do you care if I plug in my music? I can't run in silence."

The fact that she was willing to play it aloud instead of putting in earbuds made something inside him warm. He found he could really look forward to these moments of sweetness in the midst of all the tart he enjoyed. "Sure. I'm not particular about what I listen to."

"As long as it's got some *twang*, right?"

"Darlin', your prejudice is showing again."

She popped her iPod into the jack next to them. It was a token of how nice this gym was that it actually had docks for electronics instead of just an old radio like the one he frequented. Immediately a familiar strain of music came from the speakers. Brock stared. "'I'm Shipping Up to Boston'?"

Regan shrugged. "Dropkick Murphys are underappreciated."

Maybe, but he hadn't expected a poised and pretty

woman like her to have any sort of appreciation for Irish punk. She stepped onto her treadmill and said, "Seven miles an hour good for you?"

"Sure." It'd be a nice easy pace.

"Then enough chatting. Let's get to it."

He obeyed as she cranked up her speed. Soon enough, they were both jogging comfortably. It was so strange. He would have guessed that she'd need a drink to calm her nerves after that fuckup in the trees, but she'd come at him with the running thing. And now her iPod was playing Social Distortion and she was humming along under her breath, which was something he never would have expected.

Turned out there was a lot about Regan that surprised him.

And masochist that he apparently was, he wanted to stick around and find out more. It didn't matter that she seemed more than willing to write him off as a worthless POS. He had this perverse desire to prove to her that he was more than good enough for a woman like her.

They kept going, running until the miles melted away and his breath sawed through his lungs. He fell into the familiar pace, though his thoughts circled around the woman next to him.

What would it take for her to reconsider her initial judgment of him?

He didn't like the thought of having to prove himself to anyone—not after he'd been trying and failing for the last thirty-odd years with his father. It stuck in his throat that Regan so blatantly preferred Logan to him. She'd lose her damn mind if she met Caine. He was just as driven, polished, and successful as Logan. Maybe more so.

And Brock knew just how well he measured up against his brother.

Did he really stand a chance against Caine 2.0?

• • •

It took twenty minutes before Regan was finally able to think straight. And her first thought was that two gym sessions in a day was going to leave her hating life tomorrow. She took a quick swig of her water and let herself finally look at Brock in the mirror.

She'd expected him to show up in a cutoff shirt that exposed those tanned and toned up arms to perfection. But no, he wore a threadbare T-shirt that had long ago faded from black to gray, the writing on the front indecipherable from countless washings. With the faint sheen of sweat on his skin and his feet thumping the treadmill in perfect rhythm with hers, he looked like temptation.

He'd handled her.

The realization didn't sit well. She'd been about to freak the hell out when he'd come for her, and he'd known it. Instead of patronizing her or washing his hands of it—both of which she'd deserved after some of the stuff she said to him—he'd taken care of her. In a really unexpected way.

Normal people didn't offer to jog until they couldn't feel their legs just so the crazy woman could outrun her fear. But Brock had. Still was.

She glanced down. Three miles. That was good enough. She slapped the stop button and waited until he'd done the same to speak. Or maybe she was being a coward, because it was significantly more difficult to say the words than she would have expected. "Thank you."

"Don't worry about it." He flashed her a grin. "Though if you're feeling particularly grateful, I could go for a drink."

She could fall into that smile if she let herself. Enjoy this time with him and then get back to her life at the end of the week. They'd probably have a whole hell of a lot of fun.

No.

If her little freak-out earlier had proven anything, it was that when she deviated from her plan, she got into trouble.

He wasn't part of the plan. They'd had fun last night, and he'd helped her out today—in more ways than one—but that didn't mean a single thing in the grand scheme of things.

She wanted what her parents had—a true partner who loved her more than anything else in the world, supported her in her choice of career, and brought stability to her life. Which meant someone equally driven, who had the same set of goals Regan did.

Brock wasn't that.

But Logan might very well be.

She couldn't afford to miss the opportunity to get closer to Logan and see if he would be a good fit. *That* was the plan for the week. Not to lose her head—or, God forbid, her heart—over a Southern playboy with too much time on his hands.

Her control once again firmly in place, she gave him her professional smile. "Like I said, thank you for helping me out. Have a good rest of your evening."

She snatched her iPod off the dock and made it nearly to the door before he came after her. "Whoa, hold on there. I'm only talking one drink."

It was more temptation to say yes than she wanted to

admit. Because damn it, she actually kind of *liked* him even though he drove her to distraction.

Get a grip, Regan. You've dated guys like him. Only a fool gets involved with a man expecting him to change. It doesn't happen.

She wasn't a fool. So she patted his arm. "Then go ahead and get one. I'm sure you'll have plenty of opportunity for company, too, if it floats your boat."

"There's only one person whose company I'm interested in right now."

Right now. Which just went to prove her point. Brock might prefer her right now, but that could change in an instant. She might wake up one day and realize his interest had shifted to some buxom blonde or a sultry redhead overnight. She didn't need that kind of aggravation and uncertainty in her life. She couldn't live with the fear that he'd get bored and leave just like he had every woman before her.

Which just reinforced that Logan was the better option. "I'm sure I'll see you around." *As little as I can possibly manage.*

If today had proved anything, it was that she couldn't afford to spend any more time with Brock. He made her forget herself, forget what was important.

And that was unforgivable.

Chapter Seven

Brock showered and spent the rest of the evening flipping through television channels. He was tempted to cruise through the bar, get a drink and the scope of the land, but he knew it for the bullshit ploy it was.

He wanted to see if Regan was there.

It was pretty damn clear she wanted to be anywhere he wasn't, but he couldn't leave it alone. Because he *knew* she'd had a good time with him, when it came to both sex and verbally sparring. She just had her perfectly styled head all wrapped up in the idea of Logan.

So it came to that. Did he bow out? Let her throw herself at Logan, and watch them flirt for the next few days?

The thought turned his stomach. He didn't want to see her in the arms of someone else. Not to mention Logan owned a goddamn outdoors company. The man spent as much time as he could outside of the city. He free-climbed mountains for Christ's sake. What the hell did she think was going to happen the first time she followed him into the forest?

But she didn't see that. All she saw was the man's success and his charming smile and… Brock was not doing himself any favors sitting alone in his room thinking about this.

He threw on his favorite pair of jeans and a shirt and headed down to the bar. Even though he told himself not to, he scanned the room for Regan, coming up blank. There were plenty of gorgeous women and some of them even gave him clear invitations, but he made a beeline to the bar. There was only one gorgeous woman he wanted to spend any time with, and she wasn't here.

He was so screwed.

As he cut through the crowd at the bar, he was a little surprised to find Colton there alone. "Hey man."

"Hey."

He took the seat next to his friend and signaled the bartender, a pretty blonde with the practiced smile of bartenders everywhere. "Coors Light."

Colton laughed. "You can take the man out of the country, but you can't take the country out of the man."

"Can't help that I have superior taste."

"If you like your beer to taste like flavored water."

Brock smiled his thanks when the bartender slid the beer over and pretended not to notice the way she lingered, clearly willing to chat him up. "Dual purpose — I hydrate and drink at the same time."

He laughed again. "It's good to see you, Brock. We didn't get a chance to talk much the other night."

The last few days had been a hectic frenzy of planned activities with no end in sight. "You know me — same shit, different day. Napping in my office and hoping no one actually needs anything from me. Not like you, big shot. Getting married and snagging that casino contract in one fell swoop. I'm happy for you."

"Don't play the slacker role with me. You're not just floating through life like you want everyone to think. If you'd just *tell* people about the foundation, no one in their right mind would see you as a slacker."

He never should have told Colton about the Blue Boat Foundation, but he was the only person who would truly understand why Brock put his blood, sweat, and tears into the company. It was for Reed. So kids didn't have to go through what their best friend did—a mother who couldn't handle the abuse, so she left, and a father who drank too much and liked to knock his kid around.

Knock his kid around. That's how Reed described it the one time they'd talked about it. As if it wasn't that big of deal. And Brock, naive kid that he'd been, had believed him. Or at least he had until that night when he was watching his best friend bleed out from a slash to his stomach while Reed argued that he didn't need a hospital. Until he'd realized exactly what "knocking around" really meant.

The memory still made him sick. If he could spare even a handful of kids that experience, he'd move heaven and earth to make it happen. It had nothing to do with proving something, and everything to do with the helpless victims. Maybe Reed's mom would have made a different decision about leaving her boy behind if something like the Blue Boat Foundation existed back then. It could have saved his best friend a lifetime of pain and suffering.

It would have meant that a kid wouldn't have had to

watch his friend bleed and struggle to understand why Reed wouldn't go to the hospital, while he did his damnedest to stop the bleeding.

"It's not a big deal."

"That's bullshit, and you know it. Have you told your family?"

And open himself up for what would no doubt be a lecture on how his time and effort could be better spent on McNeill-owned accounts? He was sick of it. McNeill Enterprises wasn't a bad company by any means, but he was doing so much more useful work with the Blue Boat Foundation. "I think you already know the answer to that."

"You do realize that you're a little past the age of teenage rebellion, right?"

Brock laughed. "Say it isn't so." He sipped his beer. "I'm doing just fine. And this weekend is about you marrying that beautiful woman before she wises up and calls the whole thing off. Stop worrying about me."

"Go ahead, turn it around on me like you always do." Colton finished off his drink. "Thing is, we're friends. That means I have license to worry about your ass. Me and Reed, both."

"Just don't be getting any crazy ideas like an intervention. That shit's for the birds."

"You *would* say that." He laughed. "Now I'm going to go see what my beautiful fiancée is up to. Try not to have too much fun tonight."

"I'll attempt to restrain myself." He raised his beer at Colton and watched his friend make his way through the small groups of people to the door. It was good to see him happy.

Brock turned around to face the bar and took another pull of his beer. Colton was wrong. He didn't need to tell his family shit about what he was doing with the Blue Boat Foundation. If he did, it'd reek of him crawling to Daddy and begging for approval. He was better than that. Either his dad was proud of him or not, but he wouldn't whip this out of his sleeve as evidence that he was a man of worth.

He wondered what Regan would say if she knew, and inwardly kicked himself. He refused to tell her for the same reason he refused to tell his family. Either she saw him for the man he was, or she didn't, but he wasn't going to trot out proof to try to convince her.

Disgusted with himself for even considering it, he finished his beer and paid his tab. Obviously he wasn't fit company for anyone right now. He'd sleep off the mood and regroup in the morning.

Then he'd figure out what the hell he was going to do about Regan.

• • •

The minutes ticked away, dragging from one hour to the next while Regan watched the clock. Every time she closed her eyes, she saw Brock's face when he offered to let her run him into the ground so she could shake the fear dogging her steps. He hadn't had to do that.

That didn't mean she actually wanted to spend more time with the charming ass, but she could be grateful.

She glanced at the clock, cursing when only two minutes had gone by. "This is ridiculous." The damn sun wasn't even up and here she was, tossing and turning and losing sleep over a pretty man. It was like she'd transported herself back to seventh grade.

Annoyed with herself all over again, she shoved off the covers and climbed to her feet. Her muscles tightened in protest, but they weren't sore enough to keep her from the gym right now. She'd just take it as easy as possible while still burning away thoughts of a certain country boy.

Regan pulled on her last pair of shorts and tank top. If she kept this up, she was going to have to do laundry sooner rather than later. Putting the worry out of her mind—and wishing she could do the same with the rest of the thoughts circling her head—she pocketed her hotel key and marched down the hallway to the elevator. Unsurprisingly, there was no one up and about at this ungodly hour. If she was lucky, she'd have the whole gym to herself.

The elevator took long enough to get to her floor that she actually considered the stairs, but then she was on her way down. A little bit longer and the steady pounding of her feet would drive away everything pricking at her. She wished she could blame the edgy feeling making her twitchy on the scare during the scavenger hunt. It had been years since she'd set foot outside of a city, and she hadn't been prepared for how much it would shake her. She'd thought she had a handle on her intense...dislike...of nature since she'd hit a few resorts, but a beach was a far cry from all those freakish trees.

The reminder of how easy it was to make her powerless made her want to lash out just to prove she wasn't. It wasn't a rational response, hence her repeated trips to the gym. A bout of sweaty sex would work even better for getting her back into fighting shape mentally, but every time she thought of it, her mind conjured up thoughts of Brock. Falling back into bed with him would cause more problems than it'd solve, so the gym it was.

She shuddered and pushed open the door, making it three steps into the room before she realized she wasn't alone. Sophie was on the same treadmill Julie had taken yesterday morning, and the determined expression on her face made Regan wonder what she was running from—or running toward.

Maybe one day she'd actually learn to keep her nose out of other people's business… But today wasn't that day. Not when whatever Sophie's problem was might detract from hers.

She waved and stepped onto the treadmill next to her. "Hey."

Sophie did a double take. "Hey, Regan." Her gaze coasted from Regan's feet to her ponytail before she seemed to realize what she was doing and blushed. "You look different."

Which was why she didn't make a habit of socializing with people in gym getup. It wasn't great for her image. This week, she'd already run into more people than she wanted to while covered in her own sweat. Brock hadn't seemed to care, though. Hell, the look he'd given her before she walked away the last time had nearly curled her toes. And that was *after* a hard run.

Sophie turned back to her treadmill. "Sorry. That was rude. Forget I said anything."

"No, it's okay. I'm just in a weird headspace right now and not exactly fit for polite company." She rolled her shoulders and keyed up the treadmill, setting it to a fast walk to warm up. Once her muscles got going, she'd see about actually running. "Besides, I'm not one of those smug bitches who gets done up to head to the gym. If you're not sweating, you're doing something wrong."

A smile twitched the edges of Sophie's lips. "I don't think half the women at my gym got that memo."

"Mine, either. I can't figure out whom they're trying to impress. Most of them have wedding rings." And as soon as she'd started walking and chatting, the woman had relaxed a little. She still didn't look completely comfortable, but she also didn't seem like she was going to bolt out of the gym at the first sudden move Regan made. "I have a theory."

"What's that?"

"They're not trying to impress men—they're trying to prove they get banging bodies just by showing up. Women like that live on the shame of people around them."

Sophie frowned. "That seems kind of harsh."

"It is." And she'd make no apologies for that. But it was obviously time to change the subject now that she'd gotten the woman talking a little. She shot a look over. "You know, I'd suspected you were hiding a banging body of your own under those artfully baggy clothes. I approve."

She hunched her shoulders and then gritted her teeth as she seemed to force herself to stand straight. "I'm not quite there yet. Not like *you*."

"Me? Honey, I'd kill for an ass like yours." She grinned. "So, you were awful quiet the other night. Is there a groomsman you have your eye on? I think it's pretty clear Reed's spoken for thanks to our Julie, and I'm all over Bro—holy shit, I mean *Logan*, but that leaves two highly eligible bachelors." Goddamn it. Had she really just said that aloud?

She blushed again and stammered, "I-I… Why would you think that?"

"Why *wouldn't* I think that?" No need to mention that her response confirmed Regan's suspicions. Shy little Sophie had her eye on someone. "Come on, spill. I can keep a secret."

Sophie's phone rang before she choked on whatever she was about to say and she practically dived for it. "Yes?" She frowned. "When? Oh crap, that's not good. I'll be right up." She clicked off and gave Regan a worried look. "Christine and Tyler are missing."

Regan looked at her phone, but it stayed stubbornly silent. By the time she glanced back at Sophie, she was off her treadmill and heading for the door. She turned back right as she pushed it open. "It was…nice…talking to you."

"Yeah, you, too." She heard the door shut, but she was busy picking up her phone. No missed calls, texts, or smoke signals. Why the hell had Sophie been called in to help? No offense to the woman—she seemed really sweet—but she wasn't exactly toting around a Girl Scout sash full of survivalist badges. There was no way she was better in the outdoors than Regan.

But they'd called her in despite that.

She tried to be rational. Everyone and their dog knew how she felt about the woods. Obviously they wouldn't want to waste the time holding her hand when they were looking for Christine. But… She could have sat back in the lobby and bullied up some hot chocolate and coffee or something. Though Julie had most likely already taken care of it. And Kady was no doubt spearheading the search with the same tenacity that got her the big accounts. Sophie… God only knew what Sophie was there to do.

They didn't have a use for her.

It hurt, probably more than it should. Needing the distraction, she upped her speed until her tired legs could barely keep up the pace. Running herself into the ground wouldn't solve the problem, but hopefully it would give her the emotional distance she so desperately needed.

• • •

The ringing phone brought Brock out of a really fantastic dream involving Regan, naked and desperate in his bed. He cursed as he rolled over and eyed the alarm clock on the nightstand. "Somebody better be dead for them to be calling me at six a.m." He grabbed his cell phone. "What?"

"Tyler and Christine are missing. Reed's out there with the maid of honor, Julie, right now, but we need all the manpower we can get on this."

Instantly, he was awake. "How long have they been gone?"

He could hear the frustration in Colton's voice. "We don't know. Not everyone finished the damn scavenger hunt, so we just assumed they'd gone off to do their own thing. But neither of them made it to their rooms as of four this morning, and Kady is freaking out."

"I'll be in the lobby in five minutes."

"Thanks, man."

He hung up and reached for his pants. It took less than two minutes to dress and be out his door. He knew he looked a little worse for wear with his hair sticking out in all directions…and then cursed himself for caring. What did it matter if he ran into Regan? She'd already made her decision about them.

Colton met him in the lobby, Kady by his side, both looking worried. "Any word?"

"No," Kady said. The phone in her hand trilled, and she nearly fumbled it in her attempt to get it to her ear. "Yes? Oh, thank God. We'll meet you in the lobby." She ended the call. "Julie found them."

"Good." He hadn't really had a chance to talk to Tyler, but the guy seemed decent, if a little overprotective. He could get that, though. He didn't like the thought of anyone messing with Sophie.

Speaking of… Brock's attention narrowed in on her as Sophie stepped out from the shadow of the hallway to the lobby. He frowned. If he didn't know any better, he'd think she had the flushed look of someone who'd recently had sex. Yes, he could blame it on the fact she'd obviously just been in the gym…but there was a heavy-lidded look that only came from *one* thing. *What the fuck?* Who the hell was sleeping with Colton's baby sister? He'd whup their ass.

He started toward her, but then Reed stormed into the lobby, quickly followed by Julie, the maid of honor, and Tyler carrying Christine.

Immediately, all hell broke loose.

Julie was trying to plan…something, at the top of her lungs with Kady, while Reed glowered at her. Uh-oh. Brock knew that look, and it meant nothing good. Then Christine struggled out of Tyler's arms and nearly toppled when she tried to walk. He moved forward to catch her, but Tyler was already there.

Christ. Maybe he should just take a few steps back until this sorted out. He backed up and dropped into a nearby chair. There was still the question of who was desecrating Sophie, and that required his attention more than a couple of grown adults who seemed just fine, aside from Christine's ankle.

Logan wandered over with an oversize to-go cup of Starbucks and took the empty seat next to him, wincing slightly as he settled into the chair.

"Buddy, you've been spending too much time behind your fancy desk if a scavenger hunt leaves you sore." Petty, but he was feeling pretty fucking petty where Logan was concerned. What was so great about him that made Regan lose her damn mind whenever he showed up?

The worst part was that he knew *exactly* what a woman like Regan would see in Caine 2.0. He was handsome enough, successful, and polished in a way Brock had never quite managed on his best day.

"Yeah," Logan said, and shot a look toward Sophie. "It's like someone kicked my ass and left me for dead." Sophie blushed and hustled over to the group fussing over Christine.

Holy shit, *Logan* and Sophie? He'd already fantasized about slugging the guy in his too-pretty face, and now the urge turned tangible…except Logan's eyes followed Sophie across the room, and there was something in his look beyond conquest or lust. Something unsettled and, well, fuck it, captured. *Yeah, you recognize it because you stared at the same goddamn pathetic look in your mirror this morning.*

He pushed that thought out of his head, and put the impulse to do bodily harm on hold. Frankly, Logan falling for Sophie would simplify things for *him*. If he'd figured out the dynamics between those two this easily, it wouldn't be long before Regan learned the score, and then she could back the fuck off Logan's jock, thus clearing the way for him.

But if Logan broke Sophie's heart, or gave her a moment's trouble, Brock would gladly deliver the next ass-kicking, and Golden Boy would be sipping his Starbucks through a straw.

Julie spoke up, pulling him from his violent musings. "We're going to need flats for all the bridesmaids. We can't have Christine being the odd one out. Preferably silver to match the dresses." She looked around. "Where's Regan? I need my shopping expert."

Brock was moving before he made a conscious decision to. He stepped forward, putting himself in her path. It was the surest way to get her attention, and if he'd learned anything from being around Julie, it was that once she got moving, it'd take a brick wall to slow her down. "I'll find her. Silver shoes. Got it. Anything else?"

"N-no. Thank you, Brock." She patted him on the shoulder and gave him a smile that was so bright it nearly singed his eyeballs. "Bless your heart. I'm sure Regan can figure out sizes."

Southern women. Sweet as pie until they're pissed, then it's all shotguns and setting shit on fire.

"What's her room number, darlin'?"

She rattled it off, and then she was moving again, turning back to Christine. That was all the dismissal he needed. Doing his damnedest not to examine his motivation too closely, he strode to the elevators and took one up to Regan's floor. No doubt she'd be asleep at this hour, and with good reason. No one in their right minds got up with the sun when they didn't have to.

Except when he knocked on her door, she answered it

fully clothed and covered in sweat. Apparently she'd taken another trip to the gym. Regan frowned when her gaze landed on him. "If I didn't make myself clear yesterday—"

"Tyler and Christine spent the night in the woods."

"I know. I was on my way down to help find them."

"Don't worry, they're back and they're fine." He waved that away. "The long and short of it is that Julie sent me to ask you to buy bridesmaids' shoes in silver. And flat."

She rubbed a hand over her face. "Shopping. I can do shopping. I need to shower and eat something—no stores will be open for a few hours anyway."

"Great. I'll do the same and meet you back here in an hour for breakfast."

"Not necessary. This constitutes an emergency, and you'll only slow me down."

Brock laughed. "If I slow you down, drinks are on me tonight."

"Stop trying to get me drunk. You got laid once. That's all there is." She glanced back into her room as if searching for something, but then sighed. "I don't have time to argue about this. Be ready, or you're getting left behind."

Chapter Eight

Regan managed to power through getting ready and loading up a plate of fruit and yogurt without letting herself think too much. The list of things she wasn't thinking about only grew as time went on.

About her conflicting feelings over Brock, which led to conflicting feelings over pursuing Logan.

About the fact that not a single one of her friends had thought to call her to search for Christine. It still hurt that no one asked her for help until they needed someone to *shop*.

She picked at her food before finally shoving the plate away. A smart woman knew her strengths and played to them. Julie knew what she was doing when she asked Regan to take care of the shoes. If Christine couldn't walk well, heels were out of the question. Regan was the best woman for the job.

But it also made her feel the most expendable. Julie couldn't afford to leave the resort with the wedding coming up so quickly. Kady was the one getting freaking married. Sophie… Sophie had the nasty tendency to fade into the background, and Regan was pretty damn sure that was just the way the little brunette liked it.

Stop it. You did not just get picked last for the kickball team. These are your best friends. Stop feeling sorry for yourself.

Brock dropped into the seat across from her, his plate piled high with waffles, bacon, eggs, and sausage. He nodded, but seemed content to let her eat in peace.

Except she wasn't eating. She was indulging in a pity party.

Regan really should be too old for this shit. She was a professional. Getting her feelings hurt over something that was probably unintentional was stupid. So she made an effort to push it to the back of her mind and to eat. She needed the calories after all the time she'd spent in the gym the last twenty-four hours.

The reason for all that running was sitting across from her, and he was enamored with his bacon from the look on his face.

This was also her damn fault. If she hadn't opened that can of worms at the bar with Brock, she wouldn't be losing sleep thinking about how unbelievably good his chest looked without a shirt covering it, or how easily he made her forget herself when he got his hands and mouth on her. It was those memories—and fantasies—that had driven her into the gym at the tender hour of five-thirty.

By all rights, she should be so freaking exhausted that sex should be the last thing on her mind. It's too bad life didn't work out like that. Her hormones had minds of their own, and they were currently focused on Brock.

Stupid hormones.

Her fork scraped bare plate, and she looked down in surprise. While she'd been brooding over him and his freakishly sexy smile, she'd finished her food.

"You're done. Good. Let's go."

His plate was clean, too. She stared. "How the hell did you finish that so fast?"

"I'm a growing boy." He grinned, those laugh lines carving dents in his cheeks. Thank God she was sitting or she might have fallen over in the face of the sheer amusement in his expression. Brock turned those sparkling dark eyes her way. "You'd think you've never lived with a man."

She didn't figure now was the time to tell him she really hadn't. For Regan, college had come first, and she'd been too concerned with work and keeping the scholarships that supplemented her parents' contributions to worry about a boyfriend serious enough to live with. Not to mention if it was a choice between a guy and her sorority, she would have happily turned any boy down.

Then it'd been moving back to New York and fighting her way up in her field. With the eighty-hour workweeks, there'd barely been time to meet her local friends for a drink now and then, let alone hold down anything more serious. For God's sake, she couldn't even keep her potted fern alive.

So she pasted a smile on her face and pushed her chair back. "You're lucky you're cute."

"Maybe you're just developing a soft spot for me."

No way. She led the way out to the parking lot and looked around at the sea of vehicles. "I don't suppose you rented a car." It was a minor detail she hadn't considered.

She'd had a car pick her up at the airport so she didn't have to bother with one.

She probably should have thought of that before marching out here.

But he pressed his hand to the small of her back, guiding her to the row of cars on the left. "This way."

She didn't know what to do with this Brock. The one who had appeared yesterday after the fiasco of a scavenger hunt, and he didn't show any signs of disappearing. He was being...*nice*.

The car he led her to wasn't a car at all. She laughed, a few of the many things weighing her down disappearing. "You do nothing halfway, do you?"

"Never." He moved to open the passenger door of the huge red truck. Of course it was a truck. What kind of country boy worth his salt would drive anything as mundane as a Corolla?

If they hadn't already had sex, she'd take this opportunity to make a comment on his overcompensating for something. Too bad she knew he had nothing to compensate for. Regan climbed into the truck and dropped her purse on the floorboard. She might be more familiar with the insides of cabs than actual trucks, but even she could tell that this had plenty of aftermarket things done to it. Trucks didn't come this high out of the dealership, and the windows were definitely tinted.

He cranked over the engine and then they were off, cruising out of the massive parking lot and down the winding road to the highway that would lead into the nearest town.

They drove for a few minutes before the quiet got to her. But what could she say? *Sorry I keep turning you down, but I'm not sorry at all because you don't fit in with the plan I have for my life. Logan does.* Funny, but she'd barely seen Logan the last two days and it wasn't as if she was wasting away from the lack.

"What do you do for fun?" She was so surprised by the question, she just stared at him. Brock raised his eyebrows, that damn grin coming out. "Don't look so surprised. Unlike you, I don't make a habit of sleeping with women I don't like."

"We'd exchanged all of two words before that night. How the hell did you know if you liked me or not?"

"Contrary to popular belief, I'm not an idiot, and I'm just as good at sitting back and taking stock of a situation as Reed or Colton is. I just generally don't have the patience for it."

She was struck by the image of those three boys raising hell. From what she'd gleaned from Sophie, Colton and his little sister spent their summers in Tennessee, which was where he met Reed and Brock. What a trio that must have made, Colton with his schemes, Reed knocking heads together and brooding, and Brock... Well, she suspected Brock was content to just be along for the ride.

For the first time, she wondered if that wasn't by choice rather than laziness. If he spent all his time with those other two strong personalities, he couldn't possibly be as big of a waste of space as she'd originally thought. Could he?

She shifted, aware she'd been quiet too long. "Fine. I'll play. How did you know you liked me?"

"Because, even surrounded by other beautiful women, you stood out. You carry yourself as if you expect people to notice you, and you're obviously more than capable."

She shrugged, almost disappointed. What had she expected? So she caught his eye—she'd known that before he said anything since he wasn't the type of man to approach a woman out of boredom. It was her *job* to catch people's attention and make sure they sat still long enough to listen to her pitch. Once she had their attention, it was often child's play to convince them that they did, in fact, want the job she was offering.

Brock kept talking, interrupting her thoughts. "The crazy thing, though, is how you hold yourself apart. It's obvious you've busted ass to get where you are—you don't have the look of old money, but your clothes are all name-brand. Could be credit card debt, but someone as independent as you are isn't going to let herself be beholden to *anyone*, let alone some company. So I'd say you're a workaholic, but you must love your job because you don't have that overworked, burned-out look." He paused. "I'd reckon you're pretty damn lonely, too. All your friends live in different states, and a work ethic like that doesn't lend itself to a whole lot of free time."

She could only stare. Her friends knew bits and pieces of that, but they'd known her for a million years. She'd never once had a near stranger come in and strip her bare like this. Frankly, she wasn't sure she liked it. "That's a whole lot of assumptions."

"Not really. Like I said, I'm not stupid and I'm also not blind. You can tell a lot about a person just by watching for a little bit."

It was a trick she knew well since she used it often enough. She was just surprised by how *much* he'd seen. It was something she might expect from Reed—that man had the flavor of someone who saw everything—but not happy-go-lucky Brock.

She'd underestimated him.

Which meant she might have missed something else along the way. Regan forced a smile, hating that he had her second-guessing herself. She wasn't used to it. Once she had a plan, she ran with it. No fuss, no muss. Because she was rarely—if ever—wrong.

Except maybe she was actually wrong this time?

Chapter Nine

After another fifteen minutes of silence, Brock pulled into Edwards. After he'd given his reasons for singling her out in a crowd, Regan had retreated inside her own head. He'd been hunting enough to know when to show patience, though his father would be the first to say it was a trait he didn't have nearly enough of. That wasn't true. In reality, Brock just didn't find things worth being patient over all that often.

Regan was one of them.

The shock on her face when he spoke his piece was reward in a way. She made the mistake a lot of people around him did—she assumed that because he had a Southern accent and a laid-back attitude that it meant he had nothing occupying the space between his ears.

He was so goddamn tired of everyone around him thinking he had nothing to offer.

Even as the thought crossed his mind, he knew where the fault lay—with him. Brock was the one who decided, at the tender age of twelve, that he was done trying. He'd brought home a six-point buck that fall, so damn proud that he'd bagged a prize any adult would brag about. His father had only shaken his head and turned away, using that opportunity to inform Brock that his older brother had won a national debate or some shit.

That was the moment he realized nothing he did would ever be good enough for his father. It didn't matter that the man had two sons, each with his own strengths. All the old man was able to see was Caine, his heir in every way.

So Brock vowed to never to seek his father's approval again. He'd stopped killing himself over homework, and graduated with a B average—the ultimate disappointment, despite lettering all four years of high school in both football and track. He'd actually been courted by a few different scouts for football in college, but he'd turned them all down—which his dad had seen as evidence of his inability to commit. When it came to his old man, he was damned if he did, damned if he didn't.

"This will work." Regan's words brought him out of the ugly spot his mind had become.

"Okay." The thing was—he didn't resent his brother. His brother could have been the biggest dick in the world and lorded their father's approval over Brock. He hadn't. Hell, *Caine* had never missed one of his games or meets, even though he'd gone to college over an hour away.

Enough. The reason you're on this goddamn shopping trip is to get closer to Regan. Let go of the past and focus on the now.

She was out of the truck almost before he put it in park, jumping to the pavement in a ridiculously graceful move, considering she was once again wearing five-inch heels. He didn't know how she managed to walk in them without limping, but he appreciated it. Today they were pointed, a brilliant yellow that faded to black at the heel, and combined with her short black sundress, her legs looked about a mile long.

He wanted to see her in nothing but those fucking heels.

Taking a deep breath, Brock shut off the engine and headed into the fancy chick store she'd disappeared into. Inside, it looked as if the place had been bombed by something pink and glittery. Since he didn't see Regan cruising through the dresses at the front, he headed deeper into the store, feeling like a trespasser. Places like this weren't meant for men—that was for damn sure.

A middle-aged woman leaned against the counter with the register, flipping through a magazine. When she caught sight of him, her eyes lit up. "Well, hello there, handsome."

Brock wasn't sure how he felt about being eye-fucked by a woman the same age as his mother, but he was leaning toward traumatized. He took a step back when she made as if to come around the counter. "I'm just looking for my friend, ma'am."

If anything, her expression became more avid. "Oh my, what an accent you have."

Damn it. Where the hell was Regan? He cast a glance around, but she was nowhere to be seen. She wouldn't bolt through the back and leave him to the tender mercy of this saleswoman, would she?

Holy shit, she definitely would.

He started for the front door, determined to wait this out in the car, but the saleswoman somehow appeared in front of him. She smiled as she moved in closer to squeeze his arm, engulfing him in a wave of floral perfume. "Now, honey, don't be hasty. Whatever it is your friend wants, I'm sure we have it here. I'll just need some pertinent details. Like…is this a girlfriend?"

He opened his mouth to lie through his teeth, but a voice from an angel sounded at the back of the store. "Brock, baby, what's taking you so long?"

Regan sailed into view, a bright smile on her face. Only the twinkle in her eyes let him know how amusing she found his predicament. She could laugh her ass off as long she got him out of this situation without him having to scrape this woman off of him—or hurt her feelings. She swept between them, slipping her arm around his waist. "Trust my boyfriend to get lost in a sea of women's clothing. Men."

A disappointed look flitted over the saleswoman's face, but she managed a smile of her own. "Don't I know it? My ex-husband hated places like this—wouldn't even darken the door."

"I'm really lucky this one tolerates women things as well as he does." She gave his hip a squeeze, as if he were a cute puppy—or a piece of meat. "Come along, baby. We don't have a lot of time before we have to be back for the wedding." She towed him behind her to the back wall, which was covered in women's shoes.

He dropped into the single chair in the corner with a loud exhale. "Thank you."

Regan glanced behind her. "I'm surprised you needed a save."

Normally he wouldn't have. He'd have smiled at the saleswoman, flirted a little bit, and extracted himself. But on the heels of his dark thoughts, he hadn't been able to manage even that. He didn't really want to talk about *those*, though. "Every man has his moments of being caught flat-footed."

She gave him a look that said she saw right through him, and he could only hope it wasn't the truth. He couldn't stand the thought of Regan knowing his story and thinking less of him. Or worse, pitying him. He didn't need her pity and he sure as fuck didn't need her approval.

But that was his problem—not hers. And they had developed a fragile truce this morning that he wasn't willing to break for the sake of his issues.

So he sat back and watched Regan pick through the shoe selection. She gave it a surprising amount of concentration, examining and discarding shoe after shoe. When she caught him watching, she actually blushed. "Sorry this is taking so long, but I can't pick just anything if Christine's ankle is screwed up. We need comfortable and stylish. And if this is all I can do to help, then I'm going to do it right."

"By all means." He motioned at her to continue. In reality, he didn't mind waiting. It was a welcome change from the resort and the hectic schedule of activities. That said, he was enjoying this week far more than he'd expected to—and he couldn't help but admit that was mostly because of the woman in front of him.

Then he registered what she'd just said. Brock crossed his arms and leaned back in the chair. "This is important."

She didn't look up. "So important Julie sent you instead of calling me herself."

Holy shit. If he didn't know better, he'd say Regan's feelings were hurt. She set another pair of shoes aside while he considered that. If he were pettier, he'd push at her about this, maybe tease her about her fear of the woods, but he didn't want to. She'd been actually afraid yesterday, and she was actually hurt this morning. Instead of poking at her, he wanted to comfort her.

The woman had obviously broken his mind. That was the only explanation.

"Sometimes in the middle of a chaotic event—"

"Oh God, Scarlett. You don't have to explain. I get it. I'm just having a pity party." She gave him a surprisingly soft smile. "I'm fine, but thanks for trying to make me feel better."

That smile hit him in the gut, and he could barely choke out the words, "No problem, darlin.'"

About thirty minutes later—time he desperately needed to get a hold of himself—she held up a pair. "These will work." They looked a bit like gladiator sandals—if gladiators had been into rhinestones—with a crisscross strap over the toes. The heel was solely straps that must lace up the calf. Regan dropped them into their box. "Even if Christine's ankle is swollen, these will fit. And they shouldn't hurt her more than she's already hurting."

"I think they're perfect."

"Obviously. I picked them." She laughed and handed him the box, followed by three others.

He frowned, ready to focus on anything but how good trying to comfort her had made him feel. "How do you know Sophie's size?" It made sense for her to know her friends', but she'd just met Colton's little sister.

"Oh please. Give me a little credit. She's an eight dress and I'll eat my Jimmy Choos if she's not a seven and a half in shoes."

"You amaze me."

"Well, duh. That's because I'm amazing." She led the way to the register. "We'll take these, please."

Brock stepped up and reached for his wallet. "I got it."

She shot him a look. "That's not necessary."

"It has nothing to do with being necessary and everything to do with my wanting to help. You picked the shoes. Let me pay for them."

For a long moment, it looked like she was going to argue. Then she finally sighed. "Knock yourself out."

The sales woman's fingers brushed Brock's a little longer than strictly necessary as he took the bags, and he practically shoved Regan out the door in front of him in his effort to get the hell out of there.

She couldn't stop laughing as he held the truck door open for her. "Oh my God, the look on your face. You'd think she was a whole lot scarier than a woman who looks like she'd love to make you cookies."

"Very funny."

"It is. You're a panty-dropper. You can't be surprised when women throw themselves at you."

He shut the door and rounded the front of the truck, trying to formulate his answer. She was right. He had women come on to him with some regularity. It had never bothered him before.

But then, he'd never been called a panty-dropper by the one woman he couldn't get out of his head before, either. He didn't want other women looking at him—he wanted *Regan* looking at him.

It didn't make any damn sense.

Brock climbed into the truck and stared at the steering

wheel. "I haven't left a trail of broken hearts behind me."

She raised her eyebrows. "You don't have to justify yourself to me."

Maybe not, but he wanted her to understand. "I had some wild times back in my twenties—maybe more than my fair share—but I haven't been part of that lifestyle for years now. I don't sleep around. I don't drink more than a few beers here and there. I haven't—" He cut himself off before he could blurt out that he hadn't been with anyone in months. Not until Regan.

The amusement fled her face. "I'm not your mommy. I don't care if you were with a different woman every night for the last ten years."

But the fucked-up thing was that he *wanted* her to care. Because if she didn't care about any women he'd been with it was because she didn't care about *him,* and hell if that truth didn't stick in his throat.

Brock threw the truck into gear and pulled out of the parking lot, a slow simmering frustration making him grip the wheel too tight. He wanted. Christ, but he wanted.

Regan made a strange noise. "Okay, that was a lie." She rushed on before he could question her. "I do care. I hate that I do, but I care if you banged your way through an army of sluts." She took a shuddering breath. "I'm…I'm glad you haven't."

He jerked the wheel into the first side street he saw, driving down it until there was no risk of someone walking by casually. He slammed the truck into park and turned to her. "I haven't touched anyone in months. And I'm glad that you care." Then he hauled her across the seat and into his lap.

Chapter Ten

Regan didn't know what possessed her to open her mouth and spill, but she'd taken one look at the vulnerability on Brock's face and all her walls came crashing down. This man, a man who seemed to actually *see* her, had just bared a part of himself. She couldn't let her smart-ass comment stand. It wasn't fair.

Having him haul ass down a side street and yank her into his lap was just icing on the cake.

She straddled him, shivering when he ran his hands up the outside of her thighs. Brock had the look of a man who was drowning and didn't give a damn. He pulled her closer and kissed her neck. "I've never given a fuck about women's clothing, but I can't stop obsessing about your goddamn shoes."

"That's good, because I've been dreaming about your stupid laugh lines." She cupped the back of his head and moaned as he fitted her hips perfectly against his so that his cock pressed against her center. "Also, this. I've spent a lot of time thinking about this."

"Mmmm. Me, too." He let go of her hip to cup her breast. "Has the running helped?"

A breathless laugh escaped her. "No. Not even a little bit."

"That's too bad." He thrust against her. "But there's a silver lining."

"Does it involve less talking?"

His grin made her so damn wet she had to struggle not to grind against him. "Talking is definitely optional."

"I like this idea." She kissed him, teasing open his mouth and drawing a moan from both of them. It didn't matter that they were in a semipublic place and could be caught by anyone walking by. It didn't matter that Brock wasn't part of her plan. Nothing mattered except getting him inside her.

He must have been thinking along the same lines because he moved them sideways and she heard the glove compartment click and then a crinkle of what she hoped to God was a condom, because the thought of stopping right now had her almost willing to throw out every single bit of common sense she had.

"Take off your panties."

She slid to the seat next to him and shimmied out of them while he unbuttoned his jeans and shoved them down. She watched him roll the condom on, greedy for the sight of him. And what a sight it was. Even mostly covered in clothing, he was a study in male perfection.

It really wasn't fair.

As Brock made as if to push her back onto the seat, she shook her head. "I want to be on top." She couldn't totally give up control, not now, when she was already compromising her plan in such a big way.

For a second, she thought he'd argue, but then he pulled her into a quick kiss. "I swear to God, woman, I'm going to make love to you good and proper before the week's out."

Not if she had anything to say about it. But now wasn't the time to tell Brock that this changed nothing between them. It couldn't. She wouldn't let it.

She moved to the side while he lay down and then climbed on top of him. As she sank onto his length, she was grateful for a whole lot more. Regan hissed out a breath as she took him in fully, rocking against him so that he rubbed all the right spots. "You feel so good."

"You have no idea."

She opened her eyes to find him watching her, and if she thought he'd shown vulnerability before, it was nothing compared to the look of naked need on his face now. Unable to deal with exactly what that meant, she closed her eyes and gave herself over to the feeling of him inside her, his hands on her hips urging her on. The sound of their ragged breathing filled the cab of the truck, and she was struck by the desire to be naked with him in a bed, to let him do all the things to her that his dark eyes promised.

It was impossible, though.

All too soon her orgasm loomed. Her strokes became jerky as she chased that feeling of wholeness blooming inside her, but Brock kept her going. "Fuck, you are so goddamn beautiful." And just like that, she was coming, her nails digging into his forearms as he slammed into her and finished with a groan.

She let herself slump onto his chest, promising that it

would only be for a few minutes. Then she'd move. In a few minutes.

He smoothed her hair, the violent beating of his heart a drum against her ear. "That was something."

If by *something*, he meant a goddamn disaster, then he was right. How was she supposed to deal with the fledgling feelings burgeoning inside her? Brock wasn't part of the plan. He may not have an army of sluts at home, but he also lacked the key things she needed in order to be in a relationship with him. A relationship only worked if two people brought the best they had to the table and, in turn, brought out the best in each other. She might be happy with Brock for a little while, and he'd sure as hell shown some drive in pursuing her, but that spark might not always be there. If her parents had taught her anything, it was that relationships took work. She wasn't sure she could risk putting it all on the line based on a handful of days. If she did and it didn't work out…

It would break her heart.

It was a shame she couldn't be sure she would avoid that outcome altogether. He already had his hooks into her. Even after so short a time, if she walked away, she was going to walk away bleeding.

Which meant it was time for some damage control.

· · ·

Brock felt the change in her body a few seconds before she spoke, and he knew what was coming. It didn't lessen the sting of her words.

"We should get back."

It was a setback, and one he should have expected. If he'd

learned anything about Regan in this short time together, it was that she didn't do anything without a plan. He wasn't part of that plan. It had to scare her to death that she felt something for him. And she did feel something for him. Her earlier declaration wasn't professing endless love—

He gave himself a mental shake as she climbed off him and rearranged her dress. Who said anything about love? That wasn't what he wanted... Was it? He pulled his jeans back into place and buttoned them, the question circling his head. He'd never felt a burning desire for a wife or kids or the so-called American Dream.

That was Caine's gig. He was supposed to be the one to marry some society girl and have a few kids who would eventually carry on the McNeill legacy. Which made him wonder if that's exactly what Regan had in mind when it came to Logan—marriage and little overachiever babies. She was only fucking Brock while she bided her time to make a move on Logan.

How the hell had he tricked himself into forgetting about *that*?

He shook his head. Stupid to lose sight of the endgame. It was on the tip of his tongue to say something to her about Logan and Sophie, but the words turned to dust in his mouth. Winning by default wasn't his style. He'd just as soon not play. Shit. He felt like he was free-falling totally out of control when it came to this woman. She threw off his game, made him want things he had no business wanting.

It was definitely time to head back to the resort. He put the truck into gear. "Any more stops?"

"Nope."

"Good." Great. Less time trapped in this truck with

her. They'd been making progress, but Brock hadn't really thought what that might mean in the long term. If he was smart, he'd stay the hell away from her for the rest of the week. Chalk this up to two adults having a good time and move on with their lives.

As he pulled onto the highway, he recognized it for the lie it was. For better or worse, he couldn't leave Regan alone. If she told him to fuck off, then he'd have to respect her wishes, but he was going to do his damnedest to make sure she didn't want him gone.

He glanced at her, taking in the rigid set of her shoulders and the way she pointedly turned to the passenger window. It wasn't time to pursue this. He'd give her a little time to recoup—give himself a little time to plan his next approach— and then he'd circle back around.

They pulled into the parking lot of Beaver Creek Resort and both their phones went off. Regan reached hers first, flipped through it, and sighed. "I forgot about the dancing lessons."

Well, hell, he had, too. "When?"

"An hour." She reached for her door. "I wouldn't be late if I were you. Julie will hunt you down and then you're totally screwed." Then she was gone, shoe bags in hand, striding across the parking lot.

He turned off the truck and snorted. She'd left her panties behind. Again. Was it on purpose? Brock wouldn't put it past her. One last *fuck you* to him. He scooped them up and shoved them in his pocket.

There was plenty of time to figure out the perfect opportunity to give them back to her.

Chapter Eleven

Regan took extra care with her appearance before the dancing lessons, even though her heart wasn't in it. She curled her hair, studying herself in the mirror. Perfection. The snag-Logan's-attention plan was off to a great start—if he didn't sit up and take notice today, then the man didn't have a heartbeat. And he *had* to notice her now. They were four days into this trip and she hadn't had a single chance to advance her plan because she was so busy with Brock. It was just *wrong*.

Wasn't it?

Her own heart gave a dull thud. Her morning with Brock had been good—too good. Even though he hadn't pressed her on the drive back, she was still too aware of him next to her. She'd wanted nothing more than to slide across the bench seat and tuck herself under his arm. He would have let her, too.

"Stop that right now. You know better."

She did. Men like him were a distraction. Even if they didn't mean to be. It wasn't fair and it might not be nice, but she'd worked too damn hard to get to where she was to be content with someone who coasted through life, who had doors opening to him solely because of the family he'd been born into.

Her phone rang, saving her from more endless mental circling. She practically dived for it, smiling when she saw Addison's name. "Babycakes, tell me something brilliant."

She laughed. "You must be really desperate for this info. I did a bit of digging on the two names you gave me. Everything has been emailed to you."

All the ammunition she needed to give her an edge in getting close to Logan. Too bad she couldn't bring herself to open her computer and look at it. *Later*, she promised herself. "Thank you for getting back to me so quickly."

"I should let you know that I'm considering poaching both those men for my business. They'd be a hit with some ninety percent of my female clients—and a good portion of my male ones, too."

She had no idea. Regan forced a smile into her voice. "I bet."

"I know, I know, you don't share until you have a deal in the bag." Addison paused. "Unless this is personal?"

"Addison, you know better." She hated not telling her friend what was going on, but Addison was a firm believer in soul mates. She'd made it her personal goal in life to make sure everyone she came in contact with found theirs. If she knew Regan was having such conflicting feelings over Brock, she'd be on the first plane out here to meddle.

"You're right. I just hope you're managing to have *some*

sort of fun out there."

She thought about what she'd been doing in Brock's truck earlier and tried to ignore the heat spreading over her chest and up her neck. "I'm doing just fine."

"Good! We need to get together when you're finally back in town. It's been too long."

"We will, I promise."

"I'm holding you to that. Have fun!" She hung up, leaving Regan once again alone with her thoughts. She looked at her computer one last time before making a decision and turning away. She'd read whatever Addison dug up later. There was plenty of time to insinuate herself with Logan without running the risk of being late for the damn dancing lessons.

She slipped on her red Come-Fuck-Me shoes and the memory of Brock's words rolled through her. *I can't stop obsessing about your damn shoes*. Shit. She almost changed them, but every single pair she owned screamed sex. What was wrong with that? She'd bought them because they made her feel sexy and powerful, and some days she just needed that. It wasn't her fault he loved them, too.

She grabbed the shoe boxes and made her way down to the ballroom where the reception would be held tomorrow. Everyone was already there, including Brock and Logan.

She couldn't help but compare them. Logan was so wonderfully clean-cut with his short hair and button-up shirt and slacks. He was the kind of man as at home in a corporate meeting as he was in a situation like this. And those shoulders sure filled out a suit. Damn.

Brock... Brock looked like he'd just rolled out of bed after a day spent fucking. His hair was still mussed from *her* fingers, and he looked as if he hadn't a care in the world. And why would he? He knew his place and he was content to stay there.

Pointedly not looking at him, she walked up to Logan, putting a little extra swing in her hips. He smiled down at her, and she gave him a winning smile of her own. "I believe we're partners."

"That we are."

The dance instructor—a French guy Kady had found somewhere—moved from couple to couple, rearranging hands and body placement. He reached them and gave a murmur of approval. "Very, very nice. Good height difference. Come now, you must touch *ze* beautiful woman. Seduce her with your dance. Yes, yes, like this." He nudged Logan's hand from the polite placement on her side lower to her hip, and then pushed her a little closer. "Now, waltz."

She'd never danced outside of a bar, but apparently Logan had at some point, because he effortlessly led her around the floor. Wow, the guy had some moves. But he kept looking over her head and frowning at something, so she made an effort to get the conversational ball rolling. "So, Kady tells me you own your own business? That's very impressive."

"Says the successful headhunter." He grinned. "You looking to poach one of my executives?"

She answered with a smile of her own as he spun them. So, he'd been checking up on her. That was promising. "If I were, I wouldn't tell you. That said, I don't know near enough about your company."

"Professional curiosity, of course?"

Hardly. But she couldn't out and say that she was trying

to get him to talk about himself so she could find some common ground. "Maybe I'm considering taking up mountain climbing." Not freaking likely.

"In that case, let's skip the business talk and get right to the good stuff."

"Yes, let's." The good stuff. That was exactly what she wanted… Right up until Logan started going off on the best place to take climbing lessons and all the different things she had to take into consideration before she ever left the building, let alone without an experienced climbing partner.

As they circled the room, her cheeks started to hurt from the smile she kept faking. It was made all the worse by the brightness in his eyes and the enthusiastic way he went on and on and on. Holy shit, this guy was really into the outdoors.

They spun again and she caught sight of Brock with Sophie. Regan's eyes nearly popped out of her head at the red dress the woman was wearing. It was a knockout, and it revealed the rocking figure she'd commented on in the gym earlier. Brock held her in his arms, and he had a look of such utter concentration on his face that she wanted to march across the room and slap him.

It wasn't fair and it didn't make any sense, but she hated Sophie Brooks a little bit in that moment.

"But this is all theory until you get up on the wall." Logan laughed. "I don't know much about what gyms are the best in New York, but if you ever end up on my side of the States, I'll take you up."

This was the offer she'd been waiting for, but Regan couldn't work up much enthusiasm. She didn't want to be climbing a wall—she wanted to be climbing *Logan*. Though to be honest, right now she didn't even want that.

No, the only man she wanted to climb was whirling around the room with another woman in his arms.

• • •

Brock could barely focus on interrogating Sophie when he was so distracted by the way Regan beamed up at Logan. And why shouldn't she be fucking beaming? Being wrapped up in Logan's arms was what she'd spent the last few days working toward. She was exactly where she wanted to be.

"You're going to need dental work if you don't stop gritting your teeth like that. Not to mention the tension migraines."

He turned his attention back to Sophie, still not really able to believe how she'd shown up dressed to this shindig. The red dress hugged her like a second skin, showing off a body he might have looked twice at if it wasn't attached to Colton's baby sister. "Are you sleeping with someone from the wedding party?" He wanted to hear her say it—to confirm his suspicions about Logan.

She made a choked noise. "Brock Christopher McNeill, I know you did not just ask me that." But her eyes made a quick, involuntary detour over to Logan and Regan, and snapped back brimming with the same dark, edgy emotions that swirled inside him.

Holy shit, he really *was* right in his suspicions. "Don't try that middle name bullshit. You know damn well that only works when my mother does it." He leaned in. "You know, Sophie, I'm not a stupid man."

"Could have fooled me," she muttered.

"Why does everyone keep saying that?"

"You know exactly why. You define the word *under-achiever*, which is fine. It's just what you do, even if you are wasting your potential." She cocked her head to the side, the anger leaching out of her voice. "How'd I do? I think I embodied your dad pretty well."

Some of the tightness in his chest evaporated. She'd just been joking. That wasn't what she really thought of him. "He's a bastard."

"And he's never seen you for what you are. His loss." She sent another turbulent look over his shoulder and muttered, "A lot of people are losing tonight."

"Don't think for a second that you've distracted me. I want to know what's going on with you. You show up to find Christine and Tyler looking like you've been rolling around in the sheets, and now this dress."

She looked down. "What's wrong with this dress?"

He bit back a sharp reply. In all the years he'd known her, she'd never taken much interest in prettying herself up. Which she didn't need to—he'd always thought she was cute in a little-sibling kind of way. But he really would be a bastard if he cut her down right now. "There's nothing wrong with it. It's a stunner."

"Liar."

"You know better than to call me that." He spun her out and pulled her back into his arms. "What's his name?" Would she come out and say it? Sophie had a stubborn streak a mile wide, but he wanted—needed—something to distract himself from the sound of Regan's voice somewhere behind him.

"So you can run to my brother and tattle?"

"Hell no. I'll take care of this one myself." He leaned down. "Though I might bring Reed into it."

Her eyes widened. "You wouldn't."

"Again, you know better." He started to go in for the kill, but Regan's laugh rang through the hall. Brock looked over in time to see her go up onto her tiptoes and kiss Logan's cheek. His stomach dropped out, and for a second, he thought he might be physically sick. The moment passed, but the feeling remained. Beside him, Sophie hissed like an angry kitten.

Raised voices snapped his attention from Regan and Logan to where Christine and Tyler faced off. She screamed something at him and then covered her face. Tyler snarled something back, and then handed her the crutches leaning against the wall. Both Tyler and Christine left, though not together, and Kady started yelling. By the time he turned around from the debacle, Regan was gone.

The only reason Brock didn't lose his shit then and there was because Logan hadn't left. He cursed himself for being the idiot everyone seemed to think he was and stalked out. What did he expect? Regan wanted Logan and she seemed well on her way toward achieving that goal. It was exactly what she'd told him her plan was. And if he confronted her now, that's exactly what she'd say to him.

If that wasn't bad enough, now he had little Sophie to worry about. If Logan fell head over heels for Regan, she'd be crushed. Brock shook his head, going back over the look on Logan's face this morning. That wasn't the expression of a man who was just using a pretty girl for sex. There was a whole lot in the way of emotions behind it.

Christ, this was a shit show.

He needed some distance from this mess. And as he stormed out of the ballroom, he headed to his room to keep from doing something stupid like showing up at Regan's room and demanding she change her goddamn plan to incorporate *him*.

Chapter Twelve

Regan ran until her legs shook. She still couldn't outrun her thoughts—or the realization that Logan was seven shades of wrong for her. The man scaled the sides of cliffs for *fun*. What the fuck did he think she was—a mountain goat? The only thing Regan liked to scale was a few sets of stairs if she was feeling ambitious. If humans were meant to scale the face of death, then God would have given them claws or hooves or unbreakable bones or something.

Oh my God, I bet he likes to camp, too.

It would never work.

That truth plagued her as she staggered off the treadmill and headed for the elevator...and saw Brock coming her way, his head down. She ducked into a nearby doorway and held her breath as he passed, and then cursed herself for being a coward. But she'd seen his face after she'd planted that kiss on Logan's cheek—mostly to get him to shut up about the goddamn mountain climbing. He'd wanted to kill

Logan. And then probably drag her off to have his wicked way with her.

Since all the running still couldn't erase how good it felt to have him moving inside her, she wasn't about to trust her control when it came to that man.

Because nothing had changed.

Brock still wasn't the keeping kind, even if Logan wasn't for her. If this morning was any indication, she couldn't trust herself around him. It was that damn magnetism—he drew her in without her realizing he was doing it. Next thing she knew, she'd be in his arms and contemplating a future that could never be.

God, how she wanted that future today in the truck.

Regan ducked out of the doorway, and satisfied the coast was clear, she hurried to the elevator and up to her room. That had been too close. This place might be big enough to call itself a village, but she had a feeling the entire East Coast wouldn't be big enough when it came to putting distance between her and Brock.

She shut the door behind her as her phone went off. Regan jumped, feeling guilty even though she hadn't technically done anything. She thumbed it on to find a text from Julie.

SOS. Meet in lobby in ten

Well, shit. She glanced at the clock. This wasn't going to be pretty. She took the fastest shower of her life and barely paused to put on moisturizer before she threw on one of her slouchy dresses saved for lazy days and her pair of lowest heels. Then, with her hair up in a ponytail, she rushed down to the lobby.

Julie was already there, her toe tapping as she looked at her watch. For all that, she had a big, stupid grin on her face. Regan walked up and nudged her with a shoulder. "What's the SOS? Because I know that look on your face—you got some last night."

"More than *some*." Julie blushed. "Now, you know I don't kiss and tell. So let's just say both my pillows were warm this morning."

"Holy shit, you're in love." Something in her chest twanged at the thought. She was happy for her best friend, but she was also a little jealous. They swept into the restaurant and were quickly seated. "You know, since this is all my fault, I get maid of honor by default."

"Baby steps, Regan. Ah, there she is." Instantly, Julie was on point. "Christine, let's get some food in you. Let's see who I have to bribe to get us a proper breakfast of waffles. Comfort food is on the menu."

All it took was one look at their friend's face and she knew comfort food wasn't going to be enough to fix whatever was wrong. "What's going on?" Though she'd bet her last dollar it had to do with Tyler.

As Christine poured out her heart, Regan set aside her own personal bullshit and focused on taking care of her friend. And what a doozy *that* story was. Guess she'd been right about Christine and Tyler all along. By the end of their pep talk, Christine was ready to storm the fortress and get her man back. Regan gave her her best go-getter smile. "Go. I'll cover your portion."

Christine had barely made it out the door before Julie turned on Regan. "Something's wrong."

"Oh, no. I don't need any of your Aunt Sylvie's advice. I'm good." Julie liked to trot out her Aunt Sylvie's favorite sayings whenever presented with a problem, but Regan didn't think a quirky Southernism would help her current situation.

Julie's snort was indication enough of what she thought of that. "Whatever you say. But if you change your mind, you know where to find me."

"Snuggled up with your very own honey badger. Got it." She dodged a piece of waffle Julie threw and pushed to her feet. It was only when she reached the lobby that she realized she had no idea where she was going. Today was the only one during this week that wasn't scheduled out the ass, and right now, she kind of wished it was. At least then she'd have something to do besides sit in her room and watch soap operas.

Or she could put on her big-girl panties and face whatever it was on her computer—and the fact that the information she was dying to read had nothing to do with Logan.

Why couldn't he be less... Well, less everything that seemed determined to send her into panic attacks. He had charm to spare, and obviously had worked his ass off to get where he was, but the man's idea of a good time was engaging in life-or-death activities. She'd rather face walking the streets at midnight than have a tiny rope be all that was between her and falling to her death. All evidence pointed to him being a freaking daredevil. And who in their right mind went into the outdoors for *fun*? People invented cities full of houses for a reason.

She walked into her room and stared at her computer.

She already knew what information Addison would have dug up on Logan. He was freakishly perfect in every way that she thought mattered, but the idea of spending another minute talking to him about all his favorite activities made her want to catch the nearest cab for the airport.

So really, there was no point in even reading the information. Logan would never work, but that didn't mean Brock was any more suitable.

Yet she found herself opening her computer and bringing up her email. It was tempting as hell to flip through the various emails she'd gotten in the last few days, but she refused to be a coward. Ignoring the files marked Logan McCade, she opened the first on Brock.

As she read, she almost closed the file. It said everything she expected—he was bright and had a fantastic athletic history, though he'd never pursued sports after high school. Hell, it looked like he hadn't pursued *anything* after high school. He'd taken the job with his father's company and just…stayed there. There was no upward movement, no deals worth noting, not even a hint of scandal or anything to indicate he did more than show up and sleep at his desk every day.

For the first time in as long as she could remember, she wished she hadn't been right. But it couldn't be clearer that she was. With a sigh, she closed that file and opened the second one—and frowned.

What the hell was this?

Frowning harder, she reread the information. And then again. Regan reached for her phone and dialed without looking. Almost immediately, Addison's voice answered, "You're supposed to be having fun, remember? Not calling me."

"You made a mistake."

"Nope. You and I both know I don't make mistakes."

"Obviously there's a first time for everything. You have Brock McNeill listed as one of the owners of the Blue Boat Foundation. That's not right."

"Oh, believe me, it is. He's not listed on any of the official paperwork or announcements, so I had to do some extra special digging to find his name, but he's the sole founder."

"That's impossible." She would have known about this. The man she had him pegged for didn't own a nonprofit organization geared toward helping battered women and their children relocate. The Blue Boat Foundation had been making waves in the U.S. in the last five years because of the sheer amount of support it offered these women. Apartments in decent school districts. Entry-level jobs in whatever field they were qualified for—and schooling if they weren't—with plenty of room for advancement. Child care. A tiered system designed to help them stand on their own two feet without crippling them by taking away assistance completely. The freaking president of the United States had even come out in support, saying that the Blue Boat Foundation stepped in where the government fell short.

If Brock was part of this movement, she would have known.

Addison made a *tsk*ing noise. "I'm not wrong, and deep down, you know it."

Which meant Regan *had* been wrong. At least in part. She stared at the computer screen until it went blurry. "Thanks. I owe you more than just lunch for this."

"And then you can tell me the real reason you wanted

this info."

She should have known Addison would recognize something was up. "Deal."

"Talk to you soon." Then she was gone.

She shook her head and closed the computer. Brock had some questions to answer. Why the hell hadn't he spoken up and told her what he'd been doing behind the scenes? Knowing he was part of the Blue Boat Foundation would have been enough to shut her up and put her in her place—at least for a few minutes. It would have been *so* easy.

She wanted to know why, and she wanted to know now.

• • •

Brock turned off his shower to the sound of someone pounding on his door. He sighed and wrapped a towel around his waist. What else had gone wrong? It seemed like every time he turned around at the wedding, someone else was in the middle of an emergency.

When the banging didn't show any signs of going away, he opened his door—and nearly got run over by Regan. She shoved past him and spun. "Why didn't you tell me?"

"Afternoon." He closed the door and leaned against it, taking in the sight of her. She looked different today, not as composed and put together as normal. Her hair was pulled back and she didn't have a speck of makeup on her face. Most telling of all was the fact she wore beige heels of a normal height.

"You should have told me." She waved a hand in his face. "All this time, I thought you were something you're not, and you've been laughing at me because you are the fucking majority shareholder in the Blue Boat Foundation."

He never would have told her. Hell, the only reason Colton knew was because the man was brilliant and Brock had gone to him for advice about getting it up and running. He'd never told Reed, but for different reasons than the ones that made him keep it from his family. "What's that have to do with anything?"

"It changes things. Or it could change things." She spun again, pacing without actually moving. "And I want to know *why*."

"Why what?" He moved closer, letting some of the anger he constantly carried with him surface. "You want to know why I didn't tell you? Because I don't need your fucking approval—or anyone else's. That's not why I started the Blue Boat Foundation. Or maybe you want to know why I started it in the first place? I did it because I grew up lucky. You think I don't know that, but I damn well do. Beyond the money you seem to hate so much, I have both my parents and my dad might be a rigid asshole, but he never once touched any of us in anger."

Needing to escape the thoughts in his head, he snagged an arm around her back and towed her against him. She looked like she wasn't sure if she wanted to kiss him or smack him, but then she closed her eyes and shook her head. "I don't understand you. Do you know how freaking rare that is? Every time I think I have your number down, you go and throw something new into the mix. It's not okay."

"Would you have kept coming around if you had my number right from the start?" The question didn't come across as flippant as he'd meant it but, damn it, her answer mattered nearly as much as her caring about his dating history.

"No." She took a deep breath. "Maybe. I don't know and that screws with my head, you know? I always know what I'm going to do before I do it, because I always have a plan. You weren't part of any plan."

And that had to scare the shit out of her. Regan was more of a control freak than anyone else he'd known. Being around him must have done a number on her. "Plans change. That's life. It's not always comfortable, but sometimes it's for the best."

"Not my plans. Not until you." She shook her head. "I guess I just can't quit you."

Before he could comment on the sheer what-the-fuckery of her quoting *Brokeback Mountain* at him, she went up on her tiptoes and kissed him. This was what he'd been missing ever since they went their separate ways yesterday. Regan, in his arms. She was wearing too many clothes, but he'd fix that in a second. Right now he was content to enjoy the strangely tentative way her tongue stroked his, as if she were memorizing his mouth.

She jerked back before he could really sink into the kiss—or move them toward the bed. Her eyes were wide and she had a look on her face he'd never seen before as she shoved out of his arms. Regan's lower lip quivered. "I…I was wrong about you, okay? It's more than the foundation, though that's part of it. But I just…I can't." Then she was gone, sliding past him and out the door before he had a chance to respond.

"That went well." He closed his eyes and rubbed a hand over his face. He hadn't wanted to use the Blue Boat Foundation to get in good with Regan. That wasn't why he spent so much time and funding keeping it running. He knew it accomplished a lot and did quite a bit of good, but he'd put it into motion for women like Reed's mother. For kids like Reed had been. Not to get his father's approval, or to get laid.

He couldn't decide if it was a positive thing or not that she'd admitted to being wrong and then run, but he wasn't going to chase her down. She knew the truth. The ball was in her court now.

Chapter Thirteen

Regan could barely string two thoughts together, which definitely made her a shitty friend because she was supposed to be paying attention to the rehearsal. She'd made it up the aisle with Reed, but she'd been too distracted by the presence of Brock behind her to even come up with a snarky comment about Reed winning Julie over.

Put shortly—she was a mess.

Brock wasn't just the majority shareholder of the Blue Boat Foundation—he was the *founder*. And if the look on his face when he talked about it was any indication, it was a passion project. Considering she never would have pegged him as a man who felt passionately about *anything*, she was still trying to wrap her head around the whole thing.

But it was more than that. She'd had a hell of a time keeping away from him even before she knew the truth. How was she supposed to do it now? There was so much about Brock she found attractive, and the reasons they couldn't be together kept going up in smoke.

Her conundrum wasn't made any easier by the fact that her focus should really be on Kady and Colton as they spoke with the pastor about how the ceremony would go down tomorrow. She should be tearing up like Julie was, or at least looking happy like Christine. Instead, she was painfully aware of Brock standing next to Tyler and the distinct lack of laugh lines on his mouth.

Because he was looking at *her*.

Why should he be happy? She'd barged into his room, yelled at him, and then run away as soon as he gave a response. Like she was a little twit, throwing a tantrum because the world wasn't the way she'd thought it should be.

Nothing was turning out like she'd planned.

"Then you'll kiss your lovely bride, and I'll pronounce you husband and wife." The pastor smiled. He wore the expression well, as if he spent a lot of time grinning. And why not? A wedding was supposed to be one of the happiest moments of a person's life and he got to witness them on a regular basis. That had to be pretty great.

And she was most definitely mentally wandering because she didn't like feeling so out of her element.

She didn't know what was going to happen with Brock and her. Rightfully so, since she wasn't supposed to want *anything* to happen with them. It wasn't part of the plan, and she was *so damn tired* of worrying about the plan. If she followed the mental checklist she'd created for her future husband, she'd end up with someone like Logan. Someone perfect and driven and so fucking wonderful it made her teeth ache. A man like that wasn't going to challenge her— unless she counted being dragged out into nature and forced into death-defying activities. He wasn't going to call her on her shit, and he wasn't going to make her want things she'd never really considered important. Things like *fun*. Things like laughter, and bickering, and outstanding orgasms in semipublic places. A man like Logan wasn't going to curl her toes with a single grin, or call her a silly pet name like "darlin'" or any of the other things she so enjoyed with Brock.

All those things she'd thought to be of secondary importance suddenly didn't seem so. Could she live without the surprises a man like Brock brought? Could she spend the rest of her life knowing exactly how each day would play out?

The answer was a resounding *no*.

"Regan."

She jumped when Christine nudged her, looking up to realize Julie and Logan were already most of the way down the aisle, and Reed was watching her with an unreadable expression on his face.

Shit. She forced a smile. "My bad. I was gathering wood."

"Wool."

"What?"

Reed shook his head. "The expression is 'gathering wool.'" He offered his arm. "Shall we?"

God, she was destined to embarrass herself time and time again at this wedding. "Sure." She slipped her hand into his arm and walked down the aisle, and she could swear she felt Brock's gaze on her the entire way.

They gathered outside the door, a great group of milling people. Regan turned to find Brock to say… She didn't know what she was going to say, but it didn't matter because he found her first. His dark eyes held none of the humor she'd come to associate with him as he leaned in. "Laugh."

She frowned. "Excuse me?"

"We wouldn't want you to miss another opportunity to catch Logan's eye, darlin'. You aren't going to get a better one than right now."

She stared at him, completely at a loss for words. He still thought she was chasing down Logan. And why wouldn't he? It wasn't like she'd told him that things inside her had been shifting in his direction over the last few days, or that the last thing on her mind right now was talking to Logan. It was *Brock* she wanted to sit down and have a discussion with.

But he wasn't waiting around for her to tell him exactly that. Brock grabbed her arm in a grasp that was just shy of painful, and towed her through the group to Logan. "Hey, man."

"Hey." Logan didn't look like he'd had much sleep since the dance lesson. There were circles under his eyes, and he had a distracted air about him that Regan could understand only too well. He nodded at them, but it was painfully obvious his attention was elsewhere.

"So, has Regan told you how much she *loathes* the outdoors?"

It was like watching a train wreck in slow motion. She opened her mouth, but once again, no sound came out. It wasn't like she cared if Logan knew she hated the woods with a fiery passion usually reserved for New York drivers and things that went bump in the night, but having Brock trot it out left her feeling sick to her stomach.

Logan finally focused on them, a small smile pulling at the

edges of his lips. "I believe she hasn't had the opportunity."

She finally found her voice, cutting in before Brock could say anything else. "Not much to tell."

"She can barely take two steps into the woods without having a panic attack. It's a real shame."

She elbowed Brock, but it was like driving her elbow into a brick wall. "He's exaggerating." She couldn't care less if Logan thought she was a scared city girl, but she couldn't stay silent while her fears were being paraded in front of him.

Logan's gaze jumped from her to Brock and back again. "They can be frightening when you're not familiar with them."

"You ever read *The Girl Who Loved Tom Gordon*? That's where my head's at when I'm surrounded by trees." She laughed, though the first shivers of fear worked their way through her at the memory of the book.

"Gotta love Stephen King, but no, I haven't had the pleasure." He frowned and added, "Seems like contracts, marketing plans, and financial reports are all I ever read these days."

Well, this couldn't get much more awkward. "That's a shame." She elbowed Brock one more time for good measure and beamed at Logan. It wasn't *his* fault he'd gotten dragged into this awkward conversation. "You should definitely check it out at some point. I have to go. I think I hear Julie looking for me." And with that less-than-graceful exit, she stepped on Brock's foot and walked away from them as quickly as she could without actually running.

• • •

As he watched her walk away, Brock felt like a complete asshole. He shouldn't have manhandled her like that, but he was still so off-center after she'd run from him. Again. All he'd wanted to do was shove the truth in her face and force her to acknowledge it—she and Logan were never going to work. Hell, the man had barely taken his eyes off Sophie the entire time they'd been talking. But all that was an excuse, and standing here in front of Logan, he couldn't ignore that.

"*The Girl Who Loved Tom Gordon*, huh?"

Brock shrugged. "It's not one of his best ones, but it's pretty good." And Regan comparing her experience to *that* made him feel even more like a dick. He knew she'd been afraid, but that was a truly nightmarish experience.

"I'll have to check it out at some point. I have a book suggestion for you, too. It's called, *If You Want to Get the Girl, Try Not Being a Complete Asshole*."

They stood there for a second longer, sizing each other up. Brock could barely look at him without seeing Caine's face imposed over his. They didn't look much alike—beyond the superficial dark coloring he and Caine shared—but the way he carried himself was identical. Caine would have been just at home in this gathering as Logan seemed to be.

"I'll consider that." He couldn't even bring himself to hate the man, no matter how much he wanted to. *This* was what Regan wanted. A man at home with whatever the world threw at him. A man who had everything going for him. A man who didn't have a boatload of issues riding him.

"Do that."

"Good talking to you." He turned on his heel and walked away, not caring if he looked like an ass while doing it.

Though he wanted to talk to Regan, he moved away from

her, too. What the hell could he say, anyway? Everything had already been said. She wanted Logan. She might have fun with Brock, but that's all it was.

Disgusted with himself for chasing a woman who so blatantly didn't want to be caught, he brushed past Reed and Colton and left the room. They'd do just fine without him, and he wasn't good company right now anyway.

What he needed was some peace and quiet to get his head on straight.

Chapter Fourteen

Brock knew camping out in his room tonight of all nights meant he failed as a best friend. But he couldn't deal with seeing Regan cozy up to Logan, no matter the cause. It was just another reminder of the ways he didn't measure up, and he wasn't in the mood to have it rubbed in his face.

What was he saying? Christ, he sounded like a spoiled little brat, throwing a fit because some kid had taken his toys. Hadn't he learned a long time ago that anything worth having was worth fighting for? And what was Regan, if not something worth having?

What had started out as a challenge had turned into something else altogether. *She* challenged him, and made him want to live up to being a better man. He loved bantering with her and seeing glimpses of the woman beneath the fearless mask she wore. She was beautiful and engaging and he refused to roll over and play dead so she could keep chasing a man who wouldn't make her happy.

Not like Brock would.

He picked up his phone, thumbing through the contacts until he found Colton. He'd have Regan's number—or would be with Kady, who would. It was time to put a stop to all the circling and games and man up. As his finger hovered over the send button, someone banged on his door.

Shit. It was probably Reed or Julie or someone from the wedding party sent to bring him back downstairs. He pulled a shirt on, working on what excuse he'd make to avoid leaving the room. Saying he had a headache was weak, but it was the best he'd come up with by the time he opened the door…to the last person he expected to find. This time she didn't barrel into his room. In fact, Regan looked downright uncomfortable. "Hi."

"Hi."

She held up the six-pack with a sheepish smile. "I brought a peace offering."

The surprises just kept on coming. If he'd been a betting man, he would have laid money on her still chatting up Logan downstairs without so much as a thought for him. Brock had never been so happy to be wrong.

He stepped back and let her walk into the room, using the opportunity to drink her in. She wore the same blue dress from the rehearsal, and it wound around her in a way that made him think it would be a whole hell of a lot of fun to unwrap, along with the same pink shoes she'd had on the first night they were together. Regan took a deep breath that made her breasts strain against her dress. "I'm sorry."

Surprise number three. He crossed his arms over his chest, buying himself a moment to recover from the shock of hearing those two little words coming out of her mouth.

"Sorry for what?"

"I haven't exactly given you an easy time of it. I saw the surface and decided that was all there was to you, and that mistake is on me. Also, for using you to get Logan's attention." She shifted from side to side. "And I'm only a little sorry for doing some digging on you."

She never did anything halfway. That was for damn sure. He fought down the smile threatening as the truth hit him. She was *here*, with him. Not Logan. Not some other CEO type. Brock. "You're only a little sorry?"

"I wouldn't do anything different, but...I might have been kind of an ass about it." She lifted the beer again. "So, like I said, peace offering if you're willing to accept it. Colton said you like this shit."

There was the Regan he knew and had come to depend on seeing. He was so goddamn glad she was here. Brock finally let his smile break through. "Can't call a classic 'shit.' It's not done."

"I can and I will. But it's totally up to you if you enjoy drinking beer out of a can." She shuddered.

He moved to his bed and patted the spot next to him. "So I take this to mean you're not going to run away again." Into Logan's arms. It was almost too good to believe it was true. He kept expecting her to tense up, throw herself at him, and flee again.

"I prefer the term tactical retreat."

"I reckon you do." He grinned as she sank down next to him. "Now that we've got that out of the way... Want a beer? This gorgeous woman just brought me some in one of the best apology gifts I've ever gotten." One of the *only* apology gifts he'd ever gotten.

"Sure." She gave him a surprisingly tentative smile. "I could go for a beer."

He opened two cans and handed her one, and then they just sat there, staring at each other. In the short time he'd known her, there hadn't been anything about their interactions that was awkward, but now that they both seemed to recognize this peace between them, he didn't know what the hell to say that wouldn't damage it. All he had to do was remind himself that she was sitting next to *him*, so obviously she must prefer him. Right?

He wanted to ask her about Logan, but that was a surefire way to shoot this thing in the foot. So he went with a less dangerous topic. "Tell me about your family."

"Not much to tell. Only child, and pretty okay with it. My parents both worked their way up from nothing, and they've busted their asses to create the life they have now. I guess I learned my work ethic from them—if you want something, get your ass in gear and *get it*. If you wait for miracles to happen, you'll still be in the same spot ten years after you start."

He could see that reflected in how she carried herself now. Regan wasn't the type of woman to sit back and wait for opportunity to come knocking. It was one of the many things he liked about her. "Attending college must have been a strain on the budget."

"It was." She shrugged, though she wouldn't meet his gaze. "Even saving for eighteen years, they barely had enough to pay for a year's worth of tuition. I got scholarships, but those only go so far, too." Another shrug. "So I worked."

He couldn't begin to imagine the dedication it took to pull off what she did. "You're amazing."

"Hardly. I just make a plan and follow it. It's a system that's gotten me through workloads that have sent other people into full-on breakdowns. And I avoid distractions."

It all made sense now. Her insistence on Logan being the kind of man for her. She had taken one look at Brock and seen him as nothing more than a distraction. The kind that would have been crippling to her handling the workload she must have.

But she was here, with him, instead of off chasing Logan around the property. That spoke volumes. "Enough about me. What about your family?"

He really didn't want to go into his family, but it was only fair. Brock took a long pull of his beer. "I have an older brother."

Regan's eyes widened. "There're some serious undertones going on right now."

"Caine was always perfect growing up, and age didn't do a damn thing to alter that." He couldn't figure out why he was telling her this when he didn't talk to *anyone* about his family shit, but it felt good to get it off his chest. "That's something else you got wrong, you know. I'm not the favored son."

She was quiet for a long moment, but he could practically see her mind racing as she connected the dots and drew new conclusions. "You know, Julie had a sister who died a few years ago. To this day, her parents constantly compare her in an unfair way."

It was something he reckoned he understood all too well. Even if Caine were gone—God forbid—he would never be the son his father wanted. "I know the feeling."

"I know it doesn't mean a whole lot, but I'm sorry."

Strangely enough, it *did* mean something. "It's no big deal. Caine walks on water in my dad's eyes. Hard to compare to that."

"What's so great about your brother?"

"He's ambitious and smart and his dream has always been to take over the family business." He made a face. "He's a lot like your Logan."

"Logan is hardly *my* anything." She settled back on the bed and took a sip of her beer. "Good God, this is horrible."

"Everyone's a critic." He laughed at the look on her face. "I can call up for some wine if you want?"

"No, that's okay. I probably shouldn't be getting drunk the night before Kady's wedding. Besides, that's not why I'm here."

Finally. The answer to the question that had been plaguing him since she showed up at his door. Brock drank the rest of his beer and set it aside. "So why are you here?"

She put the beer on the nightstand and tucked her feet under her, looking for all the world like she was bracing herself to deliver some bad news. Maybe that was why it took him a full ten seconds to process the next words out of her mouth. "Okay, so here's the deal—I like you. A lot. Probably more than I should."

It shouldn't have been surprising considering all the evidence to support just that, but Brock couldn't help the shock ricocheting through him. He'd been prepared to fight tooth and nail to get her to admit what she'd just spit out. And she sat there, her shoulders slightly hunched, as if she expected him to slap her down. He couldn't have done that, even if he wanted to, so he told her the truth. "I like you, too."

"I don't think this you-and-me thing will work past this week. Even if we didn't live a couple thousand miles from each other, we come from different worlds. And how cliché is *that*?" When he opened his mouth to protest, she held up a hand. "*But*, like I said, I like you too much to walk away. So I'm willing to stop fighting it and see what happens."

If Regan put half the effort into building something with him that she had pursuing Logan, he didn't see how anything could go wrong. He wasn't about to say *that*, though. Because the truth was, not fighting something and working for it were two different things. Which meant he had a little over twenty-four hours to convince her to give this a real shot. "I'd like that."

"Good." She still looked a little wide around the eyes, and she hadn't let go of the death grip on her arms. All signs pointed toward her being half a second away from bolting again.

He wouldn't give her the excuse. Moving slowly, he hooked her around the waist and pulled her into his lap. She went tense for a breath and then relaxed into him. Brock propped his chin on the top of her head. "Want to know something, peaches?"

She laughed. "Like why a Tennessee boy is calling me peaches? Shouldn't that be reserved for Georgians?"

"I reckon you fit the description." He shifted her so that she was straddling him. It created a little distance between them, but he couldn't fault it when it gave him the opportunity to look his fill. He didn't think he'd ever get enough of just looking at her.

She licked her lips. "How's that?"

A thousand corny answers flew threw his mind, but he

didn't give voice to a single one. "You ever hear the saying 'sweet as a Georgia peach'?"

"That's not a thing."

"Sure it is." He dropped a kiss on her lips, and then each corner of her mouth. "And you, Regan, are fucking *sweet*."

She sighed as he kissed her again, taking his time in tasting her. He delved into her mouth, sliding his tongue along hers before he withdrew and nipped her bottom lip. "Want to know something else?"

Her laugh was a little breathy. "Why not?"

"I finally have you in my bed." He untied the front of her dress, letting the fabric slide over his fingers as he pulled the knot free. "I fully plan on taking advantage of it."

"Oh yeah?"

"Most definitely." He parted the fabric and slipped his hands inside, against her skin. He forgot, sometimes, that she was so small. The force of her personality seemed to fill up a room, and yet his hands felt huge against her hips. He nudged the straps off her shoulders and down her arms, loving the goose bumps that rose in the wake of his touch.

When she leaned in, he stopped her. "Ah ah, not yet. You've had your way with me twice now. Turnabout is fair play."

She huffed, but the blush that stole along her chest gave her away. She liked this. He finished taking off the dress and dropped it on the side of the bed. The bra she wore seemed designed to offer her breasts up to him, the pink lace cups shading her nipples more than covering them. The black panties didn't match, but he liked the contrast.

Not that she was going to be wearing either long.

The shoes, though, would stay. He'd already decided

that after the first night. Brock unhooked her bra and tossed it aside. Then he just looked at her, watching her nipples pebble and her breath hitch.

"If you could see the way you're looking at me right now…"

He brushed his thumb against her nipple and along the underside of her breast. "How's that?"

"I don't have the words."

That spoke volumes. Regan always had words. He cupped her breasts, enjoying the feeling of them filling his hands, and then followed the line of her sides down to her panties. Part of him wanted to draw this out and just enjoy touching her, but he felt like he'd been waiting forever to get her into his bed. "Lose these. Leave the heels."

"You don't have to tell me twice." She climbed off him and stood at the edge of the bed to slide them down her legs.

He pulled his shirt over his head and dropped it on the growing pile of clothes. Her gaze fastened onto his chest, and he could almost feel the stroke down to the fly of his jeans. Jesus. Brock stood and pulled them off, leaving him standing as naked as she was.

"It's really not fair how amazing your body is." She reached out a shaking hand to touch first his arm, then his chest, then down his stomach. "Not even a little bit."

"Come here."

Her eyes drifted closed as he wrapped his arms around her back and kissed her, trying to put the whirlwind of emotions he felt into the way his tongue stroked along hers, his hands digging into her hips, the moan he couldn't hold back when she reached between them to touch him.

But she wasn't getting away with guiding things—not

after the last few times.

With a grin, he tumbled her back onto the bed, earning a laugh. Even sprawled out, with her hair everywhere, she was a study in perfection. Regan pushed her hair out of her face. "Tease."

She had no idea. He slid down her body, taking his time exploring her, the curve of her hips, her toned ass, and those legs. Christ, her legs were enough to bring a man to his knees. He stroked her from hip to ankle once, twice, three times, until she was shaking from the near innocent touch.

"These fucking shoes. You know, I used to be a boob man, but I think you've ruined me."

"Told you so."

He took an ankle in each hand and spread her legs slowly, until she was completely exposed to him. She didn't fight, didn't argue, didn't do anything but arch her back a little to give him a better view. "You're going to keep these on." He knew he'd said it before, but Brock couldn't get over the image of her naked except for these goddamn pink heels. It was one that would be permanently imprinted on his mind.

"Mm-hmmm."

He moved back up to settle between her thighs. She was already so wet for him, he nearly groaned as he explored her with his fingers, paying close attention to what made her catch her breath and moan. Finally, the temptation was too much. He leaned down and dragged his tongue over her. Her entire body went taut, but there was no finesse or teasing now. He wanted to feel her come against his mouth and he wanted it now.

Chapter Fifteen

Regan nearly thrashed them both off the bed at the first contact his tongue made. Brock's growling laugh against her heated flesh didn't do a damn thing to calm her racing heart—neither did his hands pinning her hips to the mattress. Had she thought she was lost the first time they kissed? *This* was being lost.

She never wanted to be found.

The next lick nearly sent her to the moon. Her reactions were almost embarrassing, but she couldn't stop the sounds coming out of her mouth. She hadn't let anyone close enough to do this in a really long time, and it was painfully obvious that her body had missed the lack. Even more, this was *Brock*. Everything this man did to her made her crazy.

He sucked her clit into his mouth, laying his teeth against her. Before she could register the shift, he had her pinned with one forearm across her lower stomach, freeing up his other hand to… "Oh my God."

He stroked her with two fingers while his mouth worked her clit, the contrasting sensations nearly too much to handle. She couldn't stop her hips from trying to move with him, and his sound of appreciation only spurred her on. The pressure built, leaving her feeling as if she were frantically chasing something just out of reach.

Then Brock twisted his fingers and sent the world crashing down inside her. Even as she dug her fingers into his hair, she wasn't sure if it was to hold on to him while she was losing every bit of herself, or to keep him doing that thing with his tongue. He gentled his movements, switching to long licks, almost as if he was savoring her taste.

His next words confirmed it. "Like I said—sweet."

Regan's reply was lost as he moved up her body, pausing to nip her hip bone and flick first one nipple and then the other with his tongue. When it seemed like he was all too content to play with her breasts, she gripped his hair and pulled him up into a kiss. She tasted herself, but that was swept away with the feeling of his hands on her as he settled between her thighs.

Brock drew away enough to say, "Condom."

She nodded because she was so damn glad *he* was thinking about safety. All she could focus on was getting him inside her as quickly as possible. He was back before she had time to miss his warmth, condom in place. She half expected him to slam into her, but he hadn't been joking when he said this would be on his terms.

As she wrapped her legs around his waist, he pushed against her, his cock sliding over her clit. It wouldn't take much to change the angle, and knowing that only heightened the sensation of him sliding against her.

"You are so fucking wet."

"For you." The words slipped out, baring her soul for him the same way she'd bared her body.

From the way he stopped moving, he knew it, too. Brock propped himself on his elbows and looked down at her. There it was again, the vulnerability that had made her back away after they had sex in the truck. Well, she wasn't going anywhere now. She cupped his face, meeting those endless dark eyes, and gave him everything. "Only you."

He reclaimed her mouth as he slid slowly into her, taking his time despite the way she tried to arch to pull him deeper. She actually cried out when his hips finally met hers, the full feeling washing over her.

But he didn't move.

She grabbed his shoulders and tried to wiggle or arch or *something*, but he had her well and truly pinned. "Brock."

"Yes." He leisurely kissed her neck, as if he had all the time in the world and she wasn't in danger of coming apart around him.

"I need you to start moving."

"Not yet."

Her desperation built with every second he spent kissing her and driving her crazy by making her wait. She finally got enough leverage to slide, just a little, and that tiny movement already had sparks building behind her eyes. Right when she was teetering on the edge of oblivion, he moved.

Again, it wasn't what she expected.

He pulled out of her almost completely, and then started the slow slide into her again. She thought she might die from needing more, but that smooth movement seemed to drag him over all the right places. Then he tilted his hips and she buried her face in his neck and she screamed his name.

Up until this point, Regan felt pretty secure in her orgasms. They were great, they got the job done, and sometimes her head even spun a little.

This one blew all of them out of the water.

She blinked up at Brock, trying to make her mouth work long enough to say…something. It was a lost cause. She could barely string two thoughts together, let alone clearly convey exactly what she was feeling in that moment.

"We're not done yet, Regan." He pulled out of her and flipped her onto her stomach. Having him at her back, his hands urging her up onto her hands and knees, made her whimper. She wasn't sure she had it in her to go again.

But then he was pushing into her, and she decided she could take a whole lot more if it meant him touching her like this. And now, *finally*, he slammed into her, taking her breath away. She started moving in counterpoint, pushing back as he shoved forward, the sound of flesh slapping against flesh filling the room even as the pressure once again began building inside her.

"Oh my God." Not again. She couldn't handle another one.

He leaned forward and pushed her shoulders down, leaving her with her ass in the air and completely at his mercy. The new angle was nearly painful, but that feeling was what sent her spiraling. "*Brock*."

His grip on her hips tightened as he slammed into her one last time. He cursed. "Holy shit." She shuddered, so overcome that she couldn't manage more than that. He collapsed next to her, leaning over to kiss her forehead before lying flat on his back. "That was something."

"Yeah." She wasn't sure what else there was to say, except she was a freaking idiot for waiting this long to hand over the reins. Maybe if she'd stopped fighting herself back at the scavenger hunt she could have spent every night getting her mind blown by this sexy beast.

Every night…

She glanced at the clock on the nightstand. It was nearly eleven, plenty early enough that she didn't have an excuse not to go back to her bedroom. Shit. She bit her lip, hating that, for the first time in as long as she could remember, she wanted to spend the night with someone—and not just for another round of sex. She wanted to wrap herself up in his Southern goodness and fall asleep in his arms.

"Stay."

She frowned at him. "What?"

"I can see your mind racing. Stay with me tonight. Let me hold you."

His words so closely mirrored what she'd just been thinking that she smiled. "Okay." After all, they'd taken some huge steps forward tonight. Leaving now felt like a betrayal of that.

So she let him draw her into his arms and laid her head against his chest. The sound of his heartbeat, slow and steady, stayed with her as she drifted off to sleep.

• • •

Regan woke up with a smile on her face. The blame for that rested solely on the naked man wrapped around her. All that tan skin and muscled shoulders and… She had better stop before she worked herself up again. After having sex no less than three times last night, she wasn't sure she could take another round and still be able to perform her bridesmaid duties later today.

Brock murmured in his sleep and pressed his face into the crook of her neck, and she sighed. He might not have been part of her plan, but she was going to make room for him in her life anyway. She couldn't imagine doing anything else at this point.

They'd talked a little last night in between making love—because it *was* making love. There was no other way to describe how he'd touched her and the deep level she'd responded on. He'd made her feel priceless and cherished and taken care of. It was no easy feat, but somewhere along the way, he'd sneaked past the barriers she had up to keep everyone out.

Just before they fell asleep, they'd decided to take it one step at a time. Maybe it would work out, maybe it wouldn't... Okay, that was bullshit and she knew it. Now that Regan had gotten a taste of what it meant to have Brock in her life, she'd fight tooth and nail to keep him there.

But right now, she had bridesmaid duties to deal with. Kady and the rest of them were meeting for breakfast, and then to get their hair and makeup done, which meant she was already late. Again. She'd never worshipped being on time the way Christine did, but this showing up late was getting ridiculous.

She kissed Brock's cheek and slid out from beneath his arm. Dressing quickly, she tried to calculate how much time she had to shower and get ready before she had to meet Kady. Not enough. Oh well, it wasn't like she had to put a whole lot of effort into hair and makeup since they were getting both done professionally.

Regan slipped out of the hotel room, carrying her heels. She froze when she met Logan's gaze, several doors down. His hair was mussed and his shirt was buttoned up wrong. His eyes went wide as Sophie ducked out of the room and laid a killer kiss on his lips.

Holy shit.

The little brunette disappeared back into the room and the door shut, but all Regan could see was the shell-shocked look on Logan's face. He obviously hadn't thought anyone would be out and about to witness what just happened. Then he gave a sheepish smile and the tension building between them broke.

She gave him a thumbs-up and turned for the stairs, relief making her feel as if her shoulders just lost a huge weight. Logan wasn't any more interested in her romantically than she was him. If she hadn't been so damn determined to show him what a great candidate she'd make for a life partner, she might have noticed that he had eyes only for Sophie. Though she never would have paired them up, obviously Colton's little sister was bringing more to the table than met the eye if she was causing *that* look on Logan's face.

I bet Sophie likes to camp.

Regan shuddered and hurried up to her room. She showered and changed in record time, not bothering to do more than blow her hair dry. Even though she knew it was silly, she couldn't keep the bounce from her step as she strode down to the lobby.

There was no missing the small group of women in the bridal party. Kady looked a little shell-shocked, but the smile never left her face. Both Julie and Christine seemed just as happy—obviously the latter had worked things out with her man. Even Sophie seemed to shine a little brighter than she had when she first showed up in Colorado.

Or maybe Regan was seeing the world through rose-tinted glasses because she'd had the best sex of her life last night with a man whom she was already falling head over heels for.

Just thinking about Brock made her smile. God, she was ridiculous.

Julie caught sight of her and waved. "There you are. I thought we were going to have to send a search party."

"Can we never talk about search parties again?"

Kady snorted. "It's not every day resort guests get lost in the freaking woods. I'm sure the staff will be telling that story for years to come—and so will we."

"I'm never going to live that down, am I?" Christine cringed.

"Serves you right for going into the woods. You're lucky you didn't get murdered by a squirrel." Thinking back at her brush with death, Regan shuddered.

"I was more worried about the bears," Christine said. "I think I was convinced Tyler *was* one at one point."

Kady patted Regan's arm. "Honey, I know this may come as a shock, but squirrels aren't actually responsible for any deaths annually." She tucked her hair behind her ears. "Bears might be, though."

Bears were the threat everyone worried about. Regan knew better. "Says you. I say they just covered up the murder. I've seen that YouTube video."

Christine sighed. "I don't know why I bother. You'll never see the glamour of the great outdoors."

"Because it doesn't exist." As the other women kept ribbing Christine about getting lost, she turned to Sophie, ready to stop talking about the nightmare being surrounded by trees was. "How was your night?"

Sophie blushed a deep crimson. "J-Just fine."

"I'll bet." She leaned closer and lowered her voice. "He's a really great guy."

"I know." Sophie shot a glance at Kady. "Can we not talk about this now? I don't need my brother or the other two Amigos getting wind of it."

"Sure." Regan smiled. "I think they're all going to be plenty busy today."

"Hey, there are no secrets among friends." Julie stepped between them and looped her arms about both their shoulders. "Let's go get some food. I'm hungrier than a badger with a hangnail."

"I swear to God, Julie, half the time I don't know what the hell you're even talking about."

Chapter Sixteen

Brock hadn't been to many weddings, but he suspected they were all barely controlled chaos behind the scenes. Colton's was no exception. They made it to the chapel with what he thought was plenty of time to spare, but most of the seats were already full.

Julie appeared as if by magic and gave him a push. "Bride's mother."

As he approached the woman who looked shockingly like Kady, he heard Julie murmur to Reed, "How am I supposed to concentrate when you look like a bona fide gentleman in your bow tie?"

The look on his friend's face was one Brock had never seen before. He wasn't brooding or sitting back and watching everyone around him. He was staring at Julie with something like wonder in his eyes. As if he couldn't quite believe she was real.

Brock could sympathize.

Who knew that Colton's happily-ever-after event would be the thing that sparked both him and Reed into their own happiness?

God, he was such a sap. But spending time with Regan last night was enough to put stars in the most jaded man's eyes. The way she'd responded to him sexually, made him laugh, and challenged him... He barely knew which way was up right now.

Even waking up this morning alone hadn't been enough to damper his good mood, probably because of the pile of panties she'd left on the nightstand—all tokens of their week together. It was a wonder she had any left to wear. Hell, maybe she hadn't. He'd be sure to investigate that thoroughly at the first opportunity he had.

Brock delivered Kady's mother to her assigned seat and walked back up the aisle. And there she was, standing between Julie and Christine and shining as bright as the sun. Regan caught him watching and winked, and it felt like his heart was suddenly too big for his chest. She excused herself and made her way over to him. "Hey there."

"Hey, yourself." This was the first time he'd seen her in flats outside the gym, and he found he kind of liked that she barely reached his shoulder. "What do you say that after the ceremony, we find a quiet corner and get into some trouble?"

"Scarlett, that's the best plan I've heard all day." She ran her hand up his chest and adjusted his tie. "You look quite dapper, by the way."

"Only the best for Colton and his woman." Though if she kept looking at him like that, he'd promise to wear clothes like this every day for the rest of his life. It didn't make any sense. He'd only known this woman a few short days, but already, he couldn't imagine his life without her. Brock opened his mouth to tell her exactly that, but Julie's voice rang out. "It's time. Everyone in their places."

The ceremony passed in a blur. Kady cried and Colton choked up, and then he swept her into his arms and laid a movie-ending-worthy kiss on her. Everyone was so happy, it was a wonder the flock of birds flying overhead didn't break into song like in the fairy tales.

He shook his head at the idiotic thought and offered his arm to Sophie as they met at the altar and walked down the aisle behind Tyler and Christine—who was still limping but only slightly.

They barely made it through the doors when Julie sprang into motion, ushering the wedding party out of the room and down to where the reception was being held. The entire room was done up with blue, with a long table at the front for them.

"Hustle, people. Punctuality gets you past the pearly gates." She caught Reed's eye, and paused. "On second thought, let's just have a good time and toast the happy couple."

As people filed into the room, Brock looked for Regan. It would be a little bit before they started in on the toasts and other shit, and he wanted a few minutes alone with her.

His good mood dampened when he caught sight of her leaning against the wall behind the bridal party's table, her gaze fastened on Logan's face. As he watched, she laughed and leaned in to touch his arm. It was a casual touch, a propriety touch. A touch between people who had been intimate.

Holy fucking shit.

His stomach sank, even as he tried to tell himself that he

was blowing things out of proportion. Logan was a friendly guy. Just because he was smiling down at her like *that* didn't mean he'd had his hands on her.

He started toward them, still trying to convince himself he was being irrational. Brock got within hearing range in time to hear Regan laugh again. "I never figured you for a backdoor guy."

Backdoor guy? What. The. Fuck?

Logan actually fucking blushed. "I'd rather people didn't know about it just yet."

"Don't worry, sweetie. It'll be our little secret—especially when you seem to take such pleasure in it. And that good-bye kiss? Good Lord, I needed a cold shower, despite what I'd just been doing."

The pit in Brock's stomach got deeper. There wasn't a good way to interpret that. He'd thought Regan was finally feeling the same way he did, but she'd gone and stuck to her plan like she always seemed to. Logan. Logan was always the goal.

Not Brock.

Logan smiled, oblivious to the fact that Brock's world was breaking apart around him. "It was a fantastic kiss, wasn't it?"

The rushing in Brock's ears drowned out whatever else they said, and he was glad for it. He'd thought Regan got up early to meet with Kady and the rest of the bridesmaids. He never would have guessed she'd sneaked out of his bed and gone into Logan's.

Christ, that hurt. It hurt more than the girls who cuddled up to him in high school telling him he was never the one they wanted, more than his father's constant comparisons to his coming up short against Caine, more than anything he'd experienced, because he wasn't expecting this. Last night she'd talked about caring for him. He should have known that nothing she felt for him would get in the way of her plan to seduce Logan. He was such a fucking fool.

Unable to stand the sight of them, laughing and sharing each other's happiness, he turned on his heel and stalked out of the room. He wouldn't make a scene here, not when it was Colton's day, but he wanted to shake her and yell until this ugly feeling inside him dissipated. How the fuck hadn't he seen that she was still hung up on Logan? He'd stupidly believed she was as into him as he was into her.

He wanted to break something.

"Brock!"

Even though he knew it was selfish, he relished the coming confrontation. Regan's skin was flushed and he eyed her mouth, trying to decide if she'd been kissing Logan or not. Brock cursed himself for torturing himself thinking about it. "What do you want?"

• • •

Regan froze in mid-step. There was something wrong with his voice. Gone was the laid-back Southern gentleman, replaced by something angry. *Just go with it. Figure out what's wrong.* "Uh, you mentioned dark corners and trouble, so I thought that's where we were headed."

In all their arguing and bantering and bickering, she'd never seen Brock look so cold. His dark eyes gave nothing away, and the grin she'd come to crave was nowhere in sight. For a moment, she thought he would just walk away without another word, but then he stepped forward, the move so aggressive, she stumbled back. "I have a question for you, Regan. The entire time we were fucking, were you planning on how to use it to your advantage in snaring Logan?"

"Snaring Logan?" What the hell was he talking about? Hadn't she just thrown her whole plan out the window for him? He *knew* that. "What are you talking about?"

"I just can't get over how well you played me. Here I was, thinking that there was actually something between us, and you always intended to use me as a jumping-off point to get to the real thing you wanted. I shouldn't be surprised. It's not the first time someone used me as leverage to get to a better man." He dragged a hand down his face. "But I didn't expect it from you. I thought… " He broke off and pressed his lips together. "Never mind what I thought. It's over. Have a nice life."

She was so shocked, she let him get half a dozen steps away before she raced after him. "Oh, no you don't. You don't get to march out here, throw a tizzy, and then take off before I get some fucking explanations."

He jerked his arm out of her grasp. "I can do whatever the hell I want."

"Brock, wait!" She reached for him again, nearly losing it when he stepped out of reach. "Please don't walk away. Can't we just talk about this? *Please.*"

Ice was warmer than his expression. "There's nothing left to talk about."

Just like that, he was done. Here she was, ready to go to her knees and beg him—*keep freaking begging him*—not to leave her. And he wasn't willing to see reason. "Why are you doing this? I was willing to make this work. I was willing to compromise my goddamn plan for you!"

He flinched like she'd reached across the space between them and slapped him. "Compromise. I'm a fucking *compromise* to you."

"That's not—"

"Enough, Regan. I don't want to hear it. I'm done."

Hurt spiked through her, its poisoned barbs sinking deep. She wrapped her arms around herself as he stalked away. "So that's it, then? You're going to drop me like yesterday's trash over some imagined slight? It's not my goddamn fault that you have inadequacy issues from your dad being an asshole. How about trying to actually *fight* for something you care about instead of throwing up your hands and pretending you don't give a fuck about anything?"

He stopped at the corner and gave her a glare so scathing, she actually shrank in on herself. "I give plenty of fucks, Regan. Just not about *you*." Then he was gone, walking around the corner and out of her life.

Her throat closed and she pressed a hand to her mouth as she searched for an empty closet, bathroom, *somewhere* to hide so she didn't break down in the middle of the hallway. The ladies' restroom was the closest door and she practically sprinted in there, nearly taking Sophie out in the process.

"Oh my God, I'm so sorry." Regan's breath shuddered out, but she fought down the burning in her eyes. She wasn't going to cry. Not here, not now. Not over a man who wouldn't even sit down and talk to her about whatever the hell his problem was.

"That's okay. I really didn't want to leave the restroom anyway."

She looked around. For a bathroom, it was pretty nice—

but she doubted Sophie was hiding in here because of the decor. Pathetically grateful for the distraction, she focused on the other woman. "What's going on? Why aren't you out there with your guy?"

"Logan's hardly mine." Sophie wouldn't quite meet her eyes. "He was only spending time with me as a favor to Colton. The good news, for you, is he's no longer stuck entertaining the groom's shy little sister. He's all yours. Go for it."

She didn't want him—she probably never had. Beyond that... "I hate to be the one to break it to you, but a man doesn't ask his best friend to sleep with his baby sister."

"But—"

"And, seriously, that scorching kiss I got an eyeful of this morning when I walked by your room was nobody's version of a favor. No one can fake chemistry like that."

A line appeared between Sophie's brows. "I don't know..."

"Yeah, you do. Deep down, a girl always knows." She'd kissed plenty of guys, and not a single damn one had made her feel a portion of what Brock did. Of course, look where she ended up—hiding in the bathroom, doling out relationship advice like she was Dear Abby. The truth was, she had no right to tell Sophie to go get her man. Regan couldn't even stick with the plan she'd relied so heavily on. She'd *known* going off the deep end with Brock would bite her in the ass, but she never would have guessed that he'd sucker punch her like this.

God, it hurt.

Realizing Sophie was still waiting for her to explain, she dredged up the last strength she had. "Look, sweetie, that man is crazy about you. Take off the underdog cape you wear around like a security blanket, because it doesn't fit at all. *You* caught Logan's eye all on your own, and now *you* need to decide if you want to keep it. But if you ask me, only an idiot would let him get away just because the idea of being with him is scary. I don't know you very well, but you don't strike me as an idiot. Don't prove me wrong." She stepped back and held open the door.

Sophie stared up at her, positively shell-shocked, and Regan didn't know whether to laugh or strangle her, but at least the little brunette was moving toward the door. She almost groaned out loud when Sophie paused at the threshold and looked back at her. "You coming?"

"I'll be along."

Sophie narrowed her eyes. "Are you okay?"

Regan raised her chin and forced a smile. "Always." *Now leave so I can have my breakdown in solitude.*

It was only when she had sole ownership of the bathroom that Regan let herself slump down onto one of the chairs situated in the corner.

As she thought back, replaying the conversation with Brock, word for word, the pain inside her only got worse. He hadn't been willing to talk, hadn't stopped to wonder if maybe he was overreacting, hadn't even paused when he accused her of using him to get with Logan. Maybe she had been to begin with—and she'd been pretty honest about it— but her plan went up in flames the second they had sex.

It just took her a few days longer to realize it.

But Brock didn't care. He looked at her and saw every single person who'd ever accused him of being lazy, stupid, and less than his brother. So he'd thrown the baby out with the bathwater, because he was more willing to walk away than realize maybe there were people in the world who actually found him amazing in his own right.

There wasn't a damn thing she could do to convince him of that, though. He'd played judge, jury, and executioner on their fledgling relationship, and she hadn't even been given a vote. She'd *begged* him not to do this, and it hadn't make a bit of difference.

This never would have happened if she'd just stuck with her damn plan.

Chapter Seventeen

Brock had never been as grateful for a 6:00 a.m. flight as he was the morning after the wedding. His goddamn brain was rebelling, offering him dozens of images of Regan and Logan wrapped up in each other. Would she make the same noises for him that she did for Brock? Would she beg him to touch her, too? Would they lie in bed and laugh about what a fool he'd been to think he actually had a chance with a woman like her?

He rubbed a hand over his face. *Fuck*. He was making himself crazy over this shit. She was just a woman. What did it matter if she preferred Caine 2.0 to him? He needed to let it go and move on with his life.

Except he couldn't stop obsessing about it.

By the time his plane landed in Nashville, he was ready to volunteer for a lobotomy. Anything would be better than the memories plaguing him, mixing in with the images he was so sure were happening right now.

He made it to his car before he broke down and grabbed his phone. It only rang once before a sleepy voice answered. "What do you want?"

"Colton, I…"

Instantly, all sleep was gone from his friend's voice. "Give me a second." He murmured something to Kady and there was a rustling sound as he got out of bed.

Holy shit, he was the worst friend ever. Colton just got married last night, and here he was, calling him because he couldn't turn off his fucking brain. "Never mind. Call me when you get back from your honeymoon."

"Nice try. You wouldn't have called for nothing, so spit it out. What's going on?"

Now that he had Colton on the phone, he didn't know how to put the clusterfuck of the last few days into words. "I fell for her, man. Regan. And she was only using me to get close to Logan."

"Yeah… I don't think so. Pretty sure Logan only has eyes for my little sister." His tone conveyed exactly how thrilled he was with his friend hooking up with his little sister.

Brock shook his head, trying to catch up. "Then he's an even bigger piece of shit than I'd guessed because he was with Regan yesterday morning."

"Uh, no he wasn't. Where the hell did you get an idea like that?" Colton sighed. "No, don't bother answering. I have my suspicions. You heard something you didn't like and took off without getting the full story."

Because she said being with him was a fucking compromise. Like he was a goddamn runner's up trophy. "I—"

"Can I ask you something?"

Knowing he wasn't going to like the coming question didn't change anything. He had called Colton, and he had to listen to whatever it was his friend had to say. "Yeah."

"When are you going to grow the fuck up and get over your shit? Seriously, Brock. You're thirty-two, and the majority shareholder in one of the most successful nonprofits of our generation. And you're still so butt-hurt about your dad being a dick that you hide behind your underachiever mask and pretend you don't give a fuck about anything. Well, I'm calling bullshit."

Brock stared at the dashboard, gripping the steering wheel with his free hand so tightly that his knuckles were white. Was Colton right? He hadn't exactly put himself out there, but it was because every time he had in the past, he got kicked in the teeth for his efforts. After a while, even *he* was smart enough to stop trying. "I don't need his approval."

"You're right. You don't. So why are you still letting his opinion of you rule your life? Your brother does that and how happy is he? I know what it takes to run a corporation— Logan is living that shit right now—and he's drowning. I'd bet a hell of a lot that it's doing the same to your brother."

He'd never thought of it like that. Caine was the lucky one, the one who lived the charmed life. He'd never counted the potential costs before. "He seems happy enough."

"Maybe he does, but so do you."

The messed-up part was that Colton was right. He'd been playing at being happy for a long time. Faking it. Hell, the only thing in his life up until the wedding that kept him going was the Blue Boat Foundation, and he operated under total secrecy there. "She doesn't want me. Not really. She must have realized Logan was interested in Sophie and compromised."

"Jesus Christ, will you listen to yourself? I might not know her that well, but even I know Regan Wakefield doesn't compromise for anyone. If she was with you, then it was because she wanted to be. Take some fucking responsibility and stop with the pity party. Do you care about her?"

It was on the tip of his tongue to deny it, to take the safe route. But he'd been doing that his entire life. Maybe Colton was right and it was time for a change. He took a deep breath and told the truth. "So fucking much."

"Then go get her. You think Kady and I had an easy go of it? We didn't. We had to fight to get where we are, and I had to decide that I wasn't willing to let her walk out of my life. Are you willing to let Regan walk out of yours? Because that damn well would be a compromise for her. Hell, maybe she'll settle down with some CEO type who will want her to be a stay-at-home mom and pop out kids for him."

A life like that would kill her, slowly and surely. She loved her work, lived for her work. She needed a man who appreciated that and supported her. A man like him. Not to mention the thought of her with someone else made him want to rip the steering wheel off and toss it out the window. "You've proven your point."

"Good. Then I'm going back to bed with my beautiful wife. Call me and let me know how everything turns out."

"Will do." He took a deep breath. "And…thanks. I know it's not always easy to tell the hard truths."

Colton paused. "In that case, I have one last piece of advice. Tell Reed about the foundation. He deserves to know." He hung up before Brock could come up with a response. It was just as well. He had a lot of thinking and planning to do. He might be falling hard and fast for Regan, but he knew better than showing up on her doorstep without some kind of plan in place. She was a woman who lived for plans, which meant he needed one of his own.

• • •

Regan finished her presentation and turned to the man at the conference table. "Those are the top three candidates I have for the job. Is there one who caught your eye?"

The CFO of Geofit Enterprises stroked his mustache, staring at the now-blank screen. "Bring them all in."

She smiled. This client tended to take the cautious approach, and he was known for going with his gut when it came to how a man shook his hand. "I thought you might say that, Mr. Reid. Shall I set the meetings up for next week?"

"Do that." He stood and shook her hand. "Good work, Ms. Wakefield."

"Thank me after you find the perfect applicant for the position." One of the three she'd handpicked would fit the bill. All of the men were exactly what Mr. Reid was looking for. It was only a matter of the right personality clicking with his.

Normally, she'd be flying high at this point, knowing that this contract was all but in the bag, but she could barely dredge up more than a flicker of excitement. In the week she'd been back in New York, nothing could touch the sad gray cloud surrounding her. She felt like Pigpen, but without the unfortunate filth.

Her phone rang and her heart leaped for one terrible second before she reminded herself that Brock had no reason to call her. He'd all but literally washed his hands of her. Men that walked out like that didn't typically come calling afterward.

Even under the crushing disappointment, she managed to perk up a little when she saw it was Julie. "Hey there, girlfriend."

"I've been meaning to call you for days, but life keeps happening."

"It does that." She'd picked up the phone more times than she cared to count to call her best friend, but she'd set it down each time without going through with it. Julie was finally happy. It wasn't on Regan to bring her problems to her door.

She would have loved to go grab drinks with Addison and bitch a little just to let off some steam, but Addison was juggling a few new clients and Regan doubted she'd see her for at least a few weeks. Which was a *good* thing. It was past time for both Christine and Julie to find their happiness.

That didn't stop Regan from feeling lonelier than she ever had before.

Julie cleared her throat. "I couldn't help but notice that you didn't come back to the reception after you left—and neither did Brock."

From the tone of her voice, she expected some juicy details, and Regan wished she could give them. Sadly, the truth was a whole lot more depressing. "He flipped out. Accused me of scheming to get Logan into bed."

"Wasn't that your plan?"

"Initially, yeah." She reached the street and decided to hold off hailing a cab. The walk would do her good. "I know I thought I had Brock's number down as a lazy playboy, but

I was wrong about him."

"I know."

She nearly tripped over her own feet. "What?"

"He called Reed this morning. Apparently Brock is actually the founder of the Blue Boat Foundation. And he did it for Reed." Her voice thickened. "You can't know how much that means to Reed—to both of us."

Regan couldn't believe he'd told Reed, not when he'd basically ripped her a new one when she found out. From that reaction alone, she would have guessed he kept his involvement on the down-low—and that was without knowing how he'd covered his tracks as much as possible so he wasn't linked to the foundation publicly. It was a mystery—and it'd remain that way because he wasn't exactly breaking down her door to confess his reasoning to her. "I know. I did a background search on him and found out he was attached to the Blue Boat Foundation."

Julie was silent for all of a beat. "Then what gives? He's a saint as far as I'm concerned, and even the village fool could tell that he's got a thing for you. Why aren't you banging on his doorstep and demanding he make an honest woman of you?"

"Just because he finally owned up to this with Reed doesn't mean he's ready for something like that." As much as she was coming to realize she wanted it. And not just with anyone—with Brock. He was the only person she'd ever been serious about who actually lightened the load of stress she carried around constantly. "He's got this underachiever bullshit down to a science. He's so terrified of coming up short that he's not willing to even *try*. Not even for me."

"Regan Wakefield, that's a defeatist attitude if I ever

heard one. Since when do you give up without a fight?"

"I don't know. I can't think straight when it comes to this guy. He's got me so twisted up, I have a few hives' worth of bees in my bonnet."

"Now you're speaking my language." Julie laughed. "But that doesn't change anything—you are Regan, She Who Plans and Conquers. You've brought terrifying corporate men to their knees without breaking a sweat—or missing happy hour. You're one of the youngest people in your field to make as much as you do. God, woman, you're a freaking headhunter. So...go plan and conquer."

"You weren't there. You didn't hear the utter disgust in his voice when he talked to me. He doesn't want to see my face again."

"You keep talking and all I'm hearing is a whole lot of excuses and unreasonable fear. Maybe he'll tell you to get lost...but I doubt it. Either way, there's only one way to find out, and that's not sitting on your cute ass and bitching to me about it."

"I hate it when you get all logical on me."

"Make a plan and execute it. That should be easy enough for *you*."

Regan turned the corner, her mind whirling. She could call Brock, but it was too easy to ignore a phone call and keep on keeping on with life. No, she had to do something he wouldn't be able to ignore or brush off. She smiled. "I hear Tennessee is beautiful this time of year."

"That's my girl!"

Chapter Eighteen

Brock finished typing out his resignation letter and pushed send before he could talk himself out of it. He'd never been more than a figurehead within McNeill Enterprises anyway. It wasn't as if his father would miss him.

Caine was another story.

He sent a follow-up email to his brother to explain his motivation. It might have been better to call, but he and Caine had grown apart over the last few years. He didn't know how his brother would respond, and he didn't have time for a lengthy discussion.

He had a plane to catch.

Stress should have been crippling right now. His dad never missed an opportunity to belittle him, but the old man wouldn't be thrilled with him quitting. Maybe he'd threaten to disinherit Brock. Maybe something else. At the end of the day, it didn't really matter. It wasn't as if he'd never threatened those exact things before. Before now, he'd always caved or toed the line of doing the bare minimum to get the old man off his back, and his dad had always backed down.

He was done dancing to the beat of that drummer. If realizing that was enough to push his dad over the edge and make him finally follow through on his threats, then so be it. The man had to do whatever it took for him to sleep at night.

Brock was ready to finally start living his own life.

Mercy Aalgard, the face of the Blue Boat Foundation, had been thrilled when he called. The work he'd put in up to this point had been cut down by his ability to carve out spare time around working for his father. Now he was free to devote all his time to pushing the Blue Boat Foundation to the next level. She already had office space in their headquarters in New York waiting for him.

So, for the second time in his life, he'd made a decision without worrying about what his father would think. The first had been creating the Blue Boat Foundation, but even that had been colored by what his father would think. Now he was finally leaving behind the baggage of his family and moving into the future.

He felt so unburdened it wasn't even funny.

Who knew all it would take was turning his back on his old life to set him free?

Now there was just one last thing to be put to rights. Regan. He pulled onto the highway and double-checked the flight time. Still plenty of time to get there and checked in. He hoped she'd give him the opportunity to apologize and explain before she slammed the door in his face.

Colton was right. The longer he thought about it, the clearer that became. He'd been judging her based on the actions of other important people in his life, all without giving her a chance to tell her side of the story. If he hadn't gone off half cocked at the reception, they might be together right now. He wouldn't be poking at her absence in his life, and hating the empty feeling taking residence inside him.

He wanted to try again. With his new position in New York, he'd actually be close enough to put a real effort behind it. He only hoped she didn't tell him to fuck off and then run to the police claiming stalking.

Brock shook his head. Who was he kidding? Regan wasn't the type of woman to let others fight her battles. She could have made a general in another life. If she didn't like what he had to say, she was more than capable of telling him exactly that…and kicking his ass to the curb.

His phone rang and he almost ignored it—it was probably the old man or Caine calling—but some instinct made him check the caller ID. *Holy shit.* He nearly fumbled it trying to answer. "Regan?"

"Where are you?"

"You called." He was so relieved to hear her voice it took him a few seconds to catch up with the question. "I'm in Tennessee." Where else would he be?

"No, really? And here I thought you'd flown to the moon in the last week." She took a shuddering breath, some of the strength leaving her voice. "So, did you know you live in the woods? Like *way* out here. What the hell is wrong with you? Who chooses to live surrounded by rabid animals who are only too happy to eat your face off?"

How the hell did she know… Brock slammed on his brakes and nearly fishtailed off the highway. Thank God no one else was on the road or he would have caused a wreck. "Where are you?"

"I'd think that was obvious. I'm in your front yard, engaged in a staring contest with a squirrel."

"Do not move." He jerked the wheel and flipped a bitch in the middle of the road. "I'm coming."

"I'm not moving. I'm pretty sure this little beast will go for my throat the second I do. So...hurry."

. . .

The squirrel moved, and Regan shrieked and dropped the phone, but the blasted thing just scurried up a tree. She scrambled for her phone, terrified to take her eyes off the massive trees that stretched over Brock's house. The second she did, that thing was going to attack from above. She just knew it. The entire tree shook as those little monsters ran through the branches, and she gave the phone up for a lost cause and dived onto the front porch.

At least this way she could see her death coming.

"Calm down, crazy. The squirrels are not going to murder you." She backed up until she was pressed against the front door. "Probably." If she had her phone on her, she'd call Julie and let her best friend talk some sense into her until Brock got back from wherever the hell he was. The only problem was that her phone was currently sitting out by the tree.

Even as she watched, the same squirrel scurried down the tree and grabbed it. "Oh my God." That was fine. She could just buy a new phone when she got back to civilization. That little freak could keep it.

The minutes ticked by, and she refused to take her eyes off the trees around her. She could do this. She could wait, right here, for Brock to show up. She would not wuss out and flee to her car.

Mostly because those little bastards were no doubt waiting to attack from above the second she walked out from beneath the porch.

A car came hurtling around the corner, kicking up a giant cloud of dust behind it. It skidded to a stop in front of the house, and Regan pressed a hand over her mouth as the dust caught up with the car and rolled over her. She sneezed, wishing she'd just been smart and called Brock in the first place. Why did she think it was a good idea to fly down here and show up on his doorstep unannounced?

Oh yeah, because Julie pushed her into it. She'd have to make sure to thank her best friend in the most imaginative way possible the first chance she got.

Brock threw open the car door and rushed around the front bumper. When he caught sight of her, he stumbled to a stop. "I thought you'd seen reason and taken off."

"More like a squirrel had dragged my body into the woods to feast on like it just did my phone." Now that he was here, none of the things she'd practiced saying seemed to fit. So she let herself drink in the sight of him, from the faded jeans to the black T-shirt that hugged his biceps. But no smile, and he hadn't exactly rushed over and swung her around romance-movie style, either.

He took another step closer. "I'm glad you weren't murdered by a cute forest animal."

"That means a lot to me." Good Lord, this was ridiculous. She wrapped her arms around herself and lifted her chin. She'd come down here for a reason, and it wasn't to talk about killer rodents. "I didn't sleep with Logan, or *anything* with Logan. The most action he saw from me was the waltz, and even that was pretty mild."

"I know."

She froze in the middle of planning out the rest of her argument. "What?"

"Colton told me Logan had eyes only for Sophie. So I reckon he didn't have much time for you."

"That lack of time was a mutual thing. You see, I'm pretty into this hot Southern guy. No one else will do."

He'd gone completely still, watching her with unreadable dark eyes. "Oh really? He sounds like a lucky bastard."

"Well, that's the thing. He had the wrong idea about me, and we both said some pretty shitty things, so I'm not sure he'll have me." He didn't say anything, didn't react, didn't give her a damn thing to work with, so she just kept talking. "I know the distance is going to be an issue, but I'm willing to fight for you. I need to know if you're willing to fight for me, too." Because this had to be a two-way street. She couldn't do all the work and beg him to love her.

No matter how close she was to doing just that.

"I'm moving to New York."

Regan stared, sure she'd heard him wrong. "What?"

Now Brock moved, closing the distance between them until he stood directly in front of her. "I quit my job. I'm going to officially step into the position waiting for me at the Blue Boat Foundation. It's something I should have done five years ago when I started it up."

In all her guesses over how this would play out, she'd never once stopped to consider that he'd do that. "That's… Oh my God, Brock, that's amazing!"

He smiled, the sight of those laugh lines making her knees weak. "Yeah, well, it's time to grow up and let go of my emotional bullshit. Plus, I hear there's this hotshot headhunter in New York who has a thing for Southern boys."

"Did you, now?" She couldn't take her eyes off his mouth as he leaned down.

"I screwed up, Regan. Really screwed up. I flew off the handle and accused you of all sorts of shit I had no right to. I'm so goddamn sorry. Is there any way I can make it up to you so you'll give us a second chance?"

She licked her lips. "I think there might be something wrong with your hearing, Scarlett. Because I pretty much just declared my intentions toward you. Second chances are on the books."

His lips brushed hers. "Forgive me? I'll spend the foreseeable future making it up to you."

And people said dreams didn't come true. Regan slipped her arms around his neck. "I forgive you."

He kissed her, pulling her against him, and it was even better than she remembered. Brock moved them, pinning her against his front door as he took full possession of her mouth. Before she could fully sink into the kiss, he pulled back. "I promise I'll keep you safe from nature, and I'll put your ass on a treadmill at the end of stressful days. I know you're more than capable of handling your business, but if you let me, I'll spend the rest of my days taking care of you."

"That goes both ways." She kissed him. "I'll show you the ropes of the big city. It's a far cry from this hellhole surrounded by trees."

Brock laughed. "Sounds like a plan."

"You know what also sounds like a plan? Getting me off this porch and into your bed."

"That, I can do."

Epilogue

"Hey, darlin'."

Regan looked up and forced herself to smile as Brock came through the door of their apartment. Even as distracted as she was, she couldn't help checking him out. With his slacks and fitted dress shirt that he'd partially unbuttoned at some point on the way home, he was something else. New York looked good on him.

He narrowed his eyes. "What's wrong?"

Shit. She should have known that he'd immediately pick up on her tension. She should have just called Addison to sit with her, but she hadn't been able to pick up the phone. The only person she wanted to be around was the same one she wanted to smack silly, because if her suspicions were right, this was mostly *his* fault.

Mostly.

"Regan, you're scaring me." He dropped his briefcase on the floor and came to sit next to her on the couch. "What's going on?"

"So, funny story." She tried to sound cheery, but it came out flat. God, what were they going to do? They'd only been together seven months. Seven seriously amazing months—like, almost too good to be true, amazing—but seven months all the same.

And she was about to ruin it. She took a shuddering breath. "Remember New Year's Eve?"

A faint smile caught the corners of his lips. "We drank too much and had sex in the bathroom of the bar."

Had sex *without* protection. "Yep. Six weeks ago."

She saw the exact moment he understood, his gaze dropping to her stomach and then flying back to her face. Regan held her breath, waiting for him to put some distance between them or accuse her of...something. To do *something*. Because she was half a second away from losing it completely.

But he didn't do any of that. Instead, he reached out and pressed his hand to her stomach. "A baby."

"Well, that's the thing. I'm too much of a chickenshit to take the test and find out for sure." She motioned at her purse lying on the coffee table. "I bought like five of them, but..."

"I'm glad you didn't." He pulled her into his arms. "Darlin', we've got to know. Together."

She studied his face, trying to figure out which way he was falling on this whole thing. He seemed...happy? Hope unfolded in her chest, threatening to consume her completely. She'd always wanted kids, and having those kids with Brock had become part of the dream the longer they'd been together. But kids were supposed to be planned out. There were so many things to take care of, doctors to interview, *plans* to make.

Nowhere in there was she supposed to get knocked up accidentally.

"Okay." She took the test from him and walked to the bathroom. When she started to close the door, he was there. "No way."

"I'm being supportive."

"Go be supportive in the living room. I don't need the added stress of you watching me pee."

He grinned, the expression doing more to steady her than anything else. "I love you."

Would she ever be able to hear him say those words without her heart speeding up? Regan hoped not. She loved that he affected her so deeply. The hope in her chest got stronger. "I love you, too."

Then she closed the door in his face.

It didn't take long to take the test, though peeing on a stick required a hell of a lot more coordination that she would have guessed. She recapped it, washed her hands, and opened the door.

Brock hadn't moved an inch. "Three minutes?"

"A man reading the instructions? Look at you, making history." She went into his arms and rested her forehead on his chest. "I'm scared."

"Don't be." He stroked her hair. "I hope it's a little girl who looks like you and spends all our money on sparkly pink shoes."

Her laugh caught in her throat. Had she really had doubts about how he'd react? He was Brock. He loved her, and he'd never once wavered since he moved up here. Of course he wouldn't waver now. "You're not mad?"

"Darlin', it takes two to make a baby."

"We don't know that there's a baby."

"Don't we?" He hugged her tighter. "It's okay to be scared. I think we'd be idiots *not* to be. Raising a kid is no joke. But if anyone can pull it off, it's you and me, together. We make a hell of a team." She could hear the smile in his voice. "Besides, a kid with half of each of us? She'll be the coolest kid that there ever was."

"Why are you so set on a girl?"

"I'd be happy with either. But I grew up in a family of boys. It'd be wonderful to raise a little girl."

Famous last words. "Until puberty."

Brock laughed and stepped back. "It's time." He stopped in the bathroom door, his smile melting away. "Unless you don't want kids? Shit, Regan, I'm sorry. I didn't even stop to think about what you might want."

He'd do it, too. If she said she didn't want a baby right now, he'd stand by her decision, no matter how much he wanted one. Just when she thought she couldn't love this man any more, it hit her hard enough that she actually staggered. Instantly, he was there, holding her up, concern written across his face. She patted his shoulder. "I'm okay."

She straightened and headed into the bathroom. There was no decision to make—if she was pregnant with Brock's baby, she'd move heaven and earth to keep their child safe. Now they just needed to know if they were getting riled up over nothing.

But when she got to the counter, she couldn't make herself pick it up. "You look. I can't."

He lifted her, studying the little window. When he looked

at her, a big, stupid grin spread across his face. "Plus sign."

She was pregnant. Regan touched her stomach, marveling at how her world had just turned on its head, but her body hadn't changed in the slightest. "We're having a baby." She looked up, realizing that he had no idea what had been going through her mind. "If it's a girl, don't you think for a moment that I'm going to let you spoil her rotten and turn her into a little princess. She'll be a monster if we don't have some ground rules."

He let out a whoop and spun her around the tiny bathroom. "I can't promise you a damn thing, but I reckon a little spoiling never hurt anyone."

She laughed. "With our luck, it's going to be a boy who will be just as much of a hell-raiser as you and your friends were growing up."

"Why stop there? Maybe it's both."

Both? She gave him a mock glare. "We are *not* having twins."

Oh God, what if they *were* having twins? No. No way. The universe was not that much of an asshole...

Was it?

Grab the rest of the Wedding Dare series!

When four bridesmaids dare one another to find lust—or maybe even love—at the destination wedding event of the year, the groomsmen don't stand a chance. But little do the women know, the men are onto their game, and sparks will fly alongside the bouquet.

Four bridesmaids. Four groomsmen.
Five *New York Times* and USA TODAY bestselling authors. Long-carried torches, sizzling new attractions, and forbidden conquests will ensure a wedding never to be forgotten.

DARE TO RESIST
a *Wedding Dare* novella by Laura Kaye

Colton Brooks is in hell. Being trapped in a tiny motel room with Kady Dresco, the object of his darkest fantasies, will require every ounce of his restraint. She's his best friend's brilliant little sister, not to mention his competition for a lucrative military security services contract. Craving her submission is *not* allowed. But as her proximity and the memory of their steamy near-miss three years ago slowly destroys his resolve, Colton's not sure how much longer he can keep his hands off...or his heart closed.

FALLING FOR THE GROOMSMAN
a *Wedding Dare* novel by Diane Alberts

Photojournalist Christine Forsythe is ready to tackle her naughty to-do list, and who better to tap for the job than a hot groomsman? But when she crashes into her best friend's older brother, her plans change. Tyler Dresco took her virginity during the best night of her life, then bolted. The insatiable heat between them has only grown stronger, but Christine wants revenge. Soon, she's caught in her own trap of seduction. And before the wedding is over, Tyler's not the only one wanting more…

BAITING THE MAID OF HONOR
a *Wedding Dare* novel by Tessa Bailey

Julie Piper and Reed Lawson are polar opposites. She's a people-pleasing former sorority girl. He's a take-no-prisoners SWAT commander who isolates himself from the world. But when they're forced together at their friends' posh destination wedding and she's dared to seduce another man, Reed takes matters into his own hands. One night should be all he needs to get the blond temptress out of his system, but he's about to find out one taste is never enough…

BEST MAN WITH BENEFITS
a *Wedding Dare* novel by Samanthe Beck

Logan McCade's best man duties have just been expanded. Coaxing his best friend's little sister out of her shell should be easy—or so he thinks until he's blindsided by the delectably awkward Sophie Brooks. She's sweet, sexy, and brings much-needed calm to his hectic life. Soon, he's tempting her to explore *all* of her forbidden fantasies…and wondering exactly how far a favor to his best friend can go.

Acknowledgments

To God, for all the things, big and little.

To Heather Howland, for plotting a truly crazy endeavor and being the one to dial us all in and help us actually pull it off!

To Ellie, for helping me to carve a better book out of the one I first wrote.

To Diane, Tessa, Samanthe, and Laura. Well, hell. We did it. There were times when I thought there was no way this would work out, but we pulled through and made these books truly great. I couldn't have done it without you!

To the Rabble, for being just as excited about Brock as I was, and for being such a positive element through it all!

To my family, for always being supportive, even when I have to disappear for a few hours here and there because the characters in my head are calling.

And last, but never least, to my readers, for not hesitating to ask what I'm working on next. Your enthusiasm never fails to amaze me and I appreciate each and every one of you!

About the Author

New York Times and USA TODAY bestselling author Katee Robert learned to tell stories at her grandpa's knee. She discovered romance novels and never looked back. When not writing sexy contemporary and speculative fiction romance novels, she spends her time playing imaginary games with her wee ones, driving her husband batty with what-if questions, and planning for the inevitable zombie apocalypse.

www.kateerobert.com
Join The Rabble!

Discover Katee Robert's NYT Bestselling **Come Undone** *series...*

Wrong Bed, Right Guy

Prim and proper art gallery coordinator Elle Walser is no good at seducing men. She slips into her boss's bed in the hopes of winning his heart, but instead, finds herself in the arms of Gabe Schultz, his bad boy nightclub mogul brother. Has Elle's botched seduction led her to the right bed after all?

Chasing Mrs. Right
Two Wrongs, One Right
Seducing Mr. Right

Introducing Katee's new **Out of Uniform** *series!*

In Bed with Mr. Wrong

Air Force Pararescuer Ryan Flannery avoids his hometown at all costs, so he's not thrilled when he's set up on a blind date... until meets mousy librarian Brianne Nave. Her sweet curves and kissable lips are like a siren's call, but her smart mouth? Not so much. How can two people have so little chemistry outside the bedroom when they fit together so perfectly in it? Stranded in a cabin by their friends, they'll be forced to find out—if they don't kill each other first.

His to Keep

Other books by Katee Robert
The High Priestess
Queen of Swords
Queen of Wands

Printed in the USA
CPSIA information can be obtained
at www.ICGtesting.com
CBHW022332011024
15253CB00006B/108